Horror on
River Road

Roy MacGregor

An M&S Paperback Original from
McClelland & Stewart Ltd.
The Canadian Publishers

For Barbara Gibson, heart and soul of Camp Lake.

The author is grateful to Doug Gibson, who thought up this series, and to Alex Schultz, who pulls it off.

Copyright © 2001 by Roy MacGregor

Canadian Cataloguing in Publication Data

MacGregor, Roy, 1948–
    Horror on River Road

(The Screech Owls series)
ISBN 0-7710-5643-5

I. Title. II. Series: MacGregor, Roy, 1948– .
Screech Owls series.

PS8575.G84H67 2001   jC813'.54   C00-932611-1
PZ7.M2555HO 2001

We acknowledge the financial support of the Government of Canada through the Book Publishing Industry Development Program for our publishing activities.

Cover illustration by Gregory C. Banning
Typeset in Bembo by M&S, Toronto

Printed and bound in Canada

McClelland & Stewart Ltd.
The Canadian Publishers
481 University Avenue
Toronto, Ontario
M5G 2E9
www.mcclelland.com

1 2 3 4 5   05 04 03 02 01

"THANKS A LOT, PAL!"

Travis Lindsay's voice shook. He could feel the blood rising in his face, his throat stinging from the sharp rasp of his own words. He couldn't remember ever being so angry at his best friend, Wayne Nishikawa.

They were standing outside the Bluebird Theatre, Tamarack's only movie house, and Travis had his fists stabbed down as far as possible in the pockets of his Screech Owls team jacket. He was surprised at how tightly clenched they felt, like they needed to be contained before something terrible happened.

Travis had never hit anyone in his life – not even in a hockey game – but he knew, in an instant, how easily it could happen. If Nish had been standing there in his full hockey equipment, helmet included, instead of in a T-shirt and shorts with that stupid sheepish look on his face, Travis might have tried to hammer him into the ground to make his point. But all he could do was yell.

"You stupid idiot! What were you thinking?"

1

Travis knew he was headed down a useless road with that question. Nish didn't think. Nish just acted. And he had acted the perfect fool this evening.

Travis had waited all week for this movie. He and Nish had seen parts I, II, III, IV, V, VI, and VII of *The Blood Children* – "*Most Frightening Hollywood Sequels Ever Made!*" "*Two Stumps Up!*" – and finally Part VIII had arrived in Tamarack on a Saturday night in early June. They were determined to be there for the very first showing of what was sure to be a long run.

The two friends – make that *former* friends – had watched the first seven movies in the blood-curdling series in the comfort of Nish's living room. Nish had somehow convinced his long-suffering mother that there was something "educational" in movies that featured one-eyed, slimy aliens from outer space, haunted graveyards, flashing blood-stained scythes, rolling heads, exploding eyes, hideous zombies, and spine-tingling, horrific screams.

"Trav and I believe," Nish had told his poor mother, all the while winking behind her back at Travis, "that all such movies should be banned."

Mrs. Nishikawa, one of the sweetest, most naive human beings Travis had ever known, had nodded slowly as she stacked the dishes, a small smile on her face showing how proud she was of her well-meaning son.

"What we want to do," Nish had continued, as if making a speech, "is work on a school project on how harmful horror movies can be to kids." He neglected to mention that the movies were all rated AA.

Mrs. Nishikawa had thought it an excellent idea and congratulated Nish on showing such maturity. But Travis knew differently. He couldn't believe how trusting Mrs. Nishikawa could be. Did she not realize school was almost out for the summer holidays and that no one would be doing school work? He wondered if she would ever ask to see their project after they had supposedly written it up.

But Mrs. Nishikawa had never asked to see anything. She even made them popcorn and brought in cold pop as Nish and Travis happily watched one rented *Blood Children* movie after the other – something the Lindsays would never permit Travis to do – until they had enjoyed all seven.

Travis could never decide whether he really liked horror movies. He liked to be frightened, but not terrified. He liked being scared, so long as he was certain it would quickly pass. At Nish's house, Travis was able to make sure he had every safety device at his disposal: the pause button on the remote control, the washroom, bright lights in the Nishikawa living room, and, if necessary, Mrs. Nishikawa's happy, comforting face seeing him to the front door before the frantic race home – preferably before dark.

Never, however, had the boys seen a horror movie in a real theatre. It was something Travis had often imagined, with a shudder. The lights would be down. The screen would be huge. Other viewers – *strangers, their faces hidden in the dark* – would be screaming. Travis wanted desperately to go, but didn't know for sure if he could handle it.

"We'll get cigars," Nish said. "Light 'em up before we hit the box office and they'll figure we're adults."

Sure, Travis thought, a couple of miniature adults wearing peewee hockey jackets and smoking huge cigars. That'll fool them for sure.

Nish pushed, but Travis refused to detour past his grandparents' so they could "borrow" a couple of his grandfather's big, stinking old Corona cigars. Travis didn't steal. He didn't smoke. And he had no intention of looking like an idiot. What next? he wondered. False beards? Canes? Hearing aids? The two of them in walkers and wearing adult diapers?

In the end, they tagged along with Mario Terziano's older brother, who was taking his date to the new movie and thought it a lark to pay for the boys' tickets and sneak them in, as long as Nish and Travis didn't actually sit with them.

Passing for fourteen seemed to do something

to Nish. He was even more outrageous than usual. Instead of sitting quietly in a corner of the theatre where they might go unnoticed, Nish insisted they sit dead centre. While they waited for the previews to begin, he made animal sounds, shouted out "KAW–WA–BUNGA!" and "EEE–AWWW–KEEE!" and once even passed wind loudly before holding his nose with one hand and raising the other high to point straight down at Travis.

Travis slid lower and lower in his seat.

The previews did nothing to settle Nish down. He whistled and stomped and clapped his hands. He began cracking jokes about the action on screen, and when some of the audience laughed, he got even louder.

Travis hoped desperately that Nish would settle down once the main feature began, but he was out of luck. *The Blood Children: Part VIII* started, and as Travis sank ever lower into his seat, Nish seemed to grow in his.

First head that got lopped off, Nish shouted out, "*That was a no-brainer!*"

First alien that popped out of a graveyard, Nish blew a bugle charge as if the cavalry were coming.

The aliens moved on some sort of jet boots that enabled them to float just above ground, and they carried vicious scythe-type weapons that twisted at the end like an illegally curved hockey stick.

It was too much for Nish to resist. When the aliens moved in for their first civilian massacre, he leaped to his feet, cupped his hands around his mouth, and yelled, "*Go Leafs Go!*"

Once he hit on this hockey theme, Nish was lost. In the movie's very first "romantic" scene – a long, passionate kiss between a gorgeous blonde actress and a handsome soldier who turned out to be a vampire – he shouted, "*Two minutes for no neck protector!*"

Instead of screaming in terror, the theatre was howling with laughter. Nish had become part of the entertainment.

But not everyone was delighted by his contribution. At one point the theatre manager, Mr. Dinsmore, had walked slowly up and down the aisles, flashing his light along the seats. But when he passed by Nish, Mr. Dinsmore saw only what every adult in a position of authority saw: Wayne Nishikawa sitting up straight, innocent as a choirboy, hands politely folded in his lap.

The Blood Children: Part VIII was particularly gross. Severed heads flew about the screen. Arms and legs were chopped off by a madman with a chainsaw. Aliens blew up. Blood splattered against the camera, dripping down the screen.

"*Where's Tie Domi when you need him?*" Nish shouted.

When the movie slowed for some dull romantic development, Nish scooted out of his seat and made for the refreshment counter. He came back with two tall drinks and handed one to Travis, who took it and sighed deep into his seat. Perhaps the drink would shut Nish up; at least he wouldn't be able to shout with his mouth wrapped around a straw.

But Nish had no intention of drinking his huge pop. He pulled out the straw and dropped it on the floor. He twisted off the plastic lid and dropped that, too. Then, to Travis's astonishment, Nish began spilling out his drink. Travis cringed, hearing the liquid splash onto the floor.

The theatre floor, made of polished concrete, slanted downward towards the screen, so the liquid immediately ran away under the rows of seats in front.

Is he nuts? Travis wondered.

Nish began splashing in the liquid with his feet, picking up his sneakers and slapping them down hard. It sounded like he was running through a deep puddle.

"*Gross!*" Nish called out.

A couple sitting up ahead turned and stared. Nish splashed again, faking that he was disgusted. He turned around and angrily faced an innocent-looking young man sitting alone about three seats directly behind.

"*What's the matter with you?*" Nish called. "*Can't you use the bathroom?*"

The young man blinked, not comprehending. Up ahead, the young couple began scrambling. The pop had washed up as far as their feet now, and they made squishy sounds as they left their seats and hurried for the safety of the aisle. The young man reached for his girlfriend's hand and pulled her. She slipped and went down, screaming. Her boyfriend raised his fist at the startled young man sitting behind Nish.

"*You pig!*" he screamed. "*Use the washroom!*"

Travis sank even lower in his seat. He could feel the body beside him shaking: Nish, in full giggle. The young man up front, after helping his girlfriend to her feet, charged up the aisle.

Not knowing what was going on, but sure something bad was about to happen, the man behind Nish scurried out of his seat as the boyfriend came at him. There was the sound of clothes ripping.

"Fight!" Nish shouted. "FIGHT! FIGHT!"

The theatre erupted in whistles and shouts. The movie ground to a halt, the lights came on, and Mr. Dinsmore and several attendants hurried down the aisle closest to Travis and Nish. It took only a few moments to break up the fight. It took slightly longer, with the lights full on, to find out that the whole thing was a misunderstanding, that the disgusting liquid was nothing more than Sprite.

Nish's Sprite.

"*Get out!*" Mr. Dinsmore shouted at Travis and Nish. "*Get out of my theatre — both of you!*"

2

"THANKS A LOT!"

Travis was shaking, but only partly from the terror of *The Blood Children*. More than anything, he shook with fury.

Here he was, finally seeing the movie he had been looking forward to for weeks, finally, for the first time, getting into a movie without adult accompaniment, and now, with the movie not even half over, he was out on the street. Not only that, but Mr. Dinsmore, pointing a long, bony finger at Travis and Nish, had threatened to call their parents to tell them what had happened. They could consider themselves "banned for life," he said.

"Banned for *life*?" Nish had snorted as Mr. Dinsmore pulled the door shut behind them. "Banned till the next movie comes to town would be more like it. He needs our business. And he won't be telling any parents on us; he'd be the one in trouble for us being in there, not us."

Travis wasn't going to waste any more breath arguing. There was no sense trying to talk to Nish now. It didn't matter to Nish that they had missed the end of the show. For Nish, the show had simply moved out into the streets, where he was still the star and the plot was whatever he decided to do next.

Travis figured the least he could do was throw him an unexpected twist, so he turned on his heel and walked away.

"Where're you going?" Nish asked.

Travis said nothing, did not even turn to acknowledge the question.

"What's wrong with you?" Nish called after him.

Travis ignored him. Leaving Nish staring after him, he struck out for home, his sneakers sticking and snapping on the pavement from Nish's drink. He did not hear Nish's own sticky sneakers following; perhaps Nish knew better than to try to act as if nothing had happened. The two had fought a thousand times before, but this one would take longer to heal than most.

It was bright along Main Street. The lights from the stores made it feel almost like daylight. There were lots of people about, some of them carrying ice cream cones, which they licked frantically in the warm late-spring air. Travis turned his thoughts away from Nish, but he was still shaking. *The Blood Children: Part VIII* had more than lived up to its gruesome billing.

To get home, Travis had no choice but to turn off Main Street. He waited until the very last possibility, then chose what he knew would be a reasonably bright route, River Street. He looked into the cloudy sky. His father had called for a new moon – "It means good fishing," he'd said over breakfast that morning – but if there was a moon it was nowhere to be seen. How Travis wished it could be a clear and cloudless night.

River Street had good lighting, but the posts were far apart and there were no storefronts here to wash their friendly light into the street. There were more shadows than bright spots, and unlike Main Street there were no people out walking with their dripping ice cream cones.

The wind rattled the new leaves overhead, almost as if it were trying to get his attention. Travis wished Nish was with him, but he knew he couldn't go back. Besides, Nish wouldn't be there anyway. He would have headed down McGee Street and cut back across King to get home.

Travis also knew that after a horror movie Nish would stay as far away as possible from the cemetery that ran along River up from Cedar Street. No way would Nish walk past a graveyard after watching *The Blood Children*.

Travis, on the other hand, had no choice. He had to walk past the cemetery to get onto Cedar and home.

He shoved his fists deeper in his jacket pockets. He wished he could wrap his right hand around a big, weighty stone. When he was younger and afraid of large dogs, he would often secretly carry a rock in his jacket pocket, though he'd never actually had to throw one. Its heft had given him an odd comfort.

What good a rock might be against ghouls and zombies, he didn't know. No rock at all to weigh him down might be a better idea. He could run faster then. He wondered if he should be running.

The wind was picking up, moaning now in the high treetops. Up ahead, shadows flickered. A cat yowled behind one of the houses.

In another few steps Travis would be beside the Tamarack Cemetery. He swallowed hard. His throat felt dry and his tongue swollen – strange, since he, unlike Nish, had just finished drinking a huge pop. He wondered if he could scream, if he *had* to scream. He could feel his heart pounding as if Muck had just put the Owls through a hard series of stops and starts.

Someone was crying!

It was impossible to tell exactly where the sound was coming from. It was so faint, barely audible above the rustle of the leaves. For a moment Travis thought it must be the cat, or the wind through a different type of tree – but then he heard a quick choke and the sharp intake of breath.

He stopped, afraid to make a sound.

He forced himself to turn to his right and look

into the cemetery. It took a moment for his eyes to adjust. There were no streetlights here and no lighting from the graveyard. The cemetery was bordered with dense lilacs, some still in bloom, and their sickly sweet smell was thick in the night air. The smell of a funeral parlour.

Something was moving! He couldn't be sure what. He thought he glimpsed a light bouncing through the branches.

Travis felt frozen. If he ran, he would only draw attention to himself. If he stayed, his wildly pounding heart might burst. He forced himself to think: he could either bolt for the other side of the street and then double back when he came to Cedar, or he could move silently along the cemetery fence until he came to the gate, and a break in the trees, where he could see in.

He closed his eyes and took a deep breath. He let it out and took a second, and held it.

He began moving, each step as cautious as if he were walking along the ridge of a high roof.

Again, the wet choking sound of someone crying!

Travis was almost to the gate. The light was moving rapidly now, seemingly dancing on the end of a string as it moved through the branches.

He was at the gate, free of the branches and leaves of the lilac.

The light suddenly snapped off.

It was dark again, pitch-black.

It's nothing, Travis told himself. Nothing at all. He let go the deep breath he'd been holding and gulped fresh air.

Of course it had been nothing. It *had* to have been nothing. Just the sound of the wind and a flash of the moon through the branches. Or distant car lights, maybe. Or that "swamp gas" Mr. Dillinger had told them about, which people mistook for UFOs. Or just a reflection. Nothing really. Nothing at all.

Travis turned to walk away, and felt every drop of blood and every ounce of oxygen leave his body.

A boy was standing by the gate.

A boy, about twelve years old.

As pale as the sliver of the new moon just now cutting through the clouds.

Weeping.

Travis stared, his mouth open, unable to speak.

The boy wiped away the tears with the back of a thin, pale hand. He smiled, weakly.

"*Help meee,*" the boy said.

And then he was gone.

14

3

"IF YOU THINK OF THE STICK AS AN EXTENSION of your arm," Muck was saying, "you'll get the knack of it a lot easier."

Muck was standing at centre ice in the Tamarack Memorial Arena, only it wouldn't be quite accurate to refer to it as "centre ice," because below his feet was concrete. The ice had been taken out weeks before. Nor was Muck in his usual track suit. Instead, he wore a torn T-shirt, worn sneakers with no socks and no laces, and an old pair of sagging white shorts with a green stripe down the sides. The long scar from the operation that had ended his dream of playing NHL hockey was clearly visible to the sixteen kids standing around him, listening.

"And don't aim. *Think* your shots in. If you picture it happening, nine times out of ten it *will* happen."

It *sounded* like hockey. Five a side; goalies, defence, and forwards; centres and wingers; passing, shooting, and checking; practices, scrimmages, and games. But at this time of year, with Muck Munro standing there, it could never be hockey. Muck had few rules about hockey, and the Screech Owls knew them by heart. Hockey is a game of mistakes. Keep your head up. Speed wins. They call it a game because it's supposed to be fun. And no summer hockey, not ever – not with Muck Munro coaching.

Yet here was Muck, at centre "ice," surrounded by the Screech Owls.

Several of the Screech Owls players – Nish and Travis included – had asked Muck to reconsider his rule against playing summer hockey. They wanted to spend the summer together as a team. And several of the parents had volunteered to set up car pools to get the team to the few rinks in the area that kept ice going all summer.

"No," Muck had replied.

The Owls had been disappointed, and it showed on their faces.

"But you can stick together as a team," he'd added. "And I'll coach."

The Owls now looked confused.

"But–but," Fahd began, "you said, 'No summer hockey.'"

"That's correct," Muck said. "Summer is for other games, other skills."

"What other skills?" Sarah had asked.

Muck smiled. "We'll play lacrosse."

Travis had been amazed at how quickly it all came together. Some of the Owls barely knew what lacrosse was, but after Muck told them how, in some places, lacrosse was even more popular than hockey, and how almost every hockey player he'd ever known – himself included – who had tried the game had fallen completely in love with it, they began to change their minds.

What convinced them was Muck's point that the skills learned playing lacrosse would pay off later on the ice. Wayne Gretzky was a great promoter of the game, and said it was in playing lacrosse that he learned how to use the area behind the net so brilliantly to set up passing plays. Joe Nieuwendyk, who once won the Conn Smythe Trophy as the MVP of the Stanley Cup playoffs, said his astonishing ability to tip pucks out of the air and into the goal came from playing lacrosse. Bobby Orr loved lacrosse; Adam Oates, the great playmaker, loved lacrosse; and even Nish's idol – his "cousin" Paul Kariya – had played it while growing up in British Columbia.

The Owls were sold.

A few of the Screech Owls had played the game before, but never together as a team. Jesse Highboy, who pointed out the game had been invented by Natives, had an uncle who'd played on a Mann Cup championship team – "Lacrosse's equivalent of the Stanley Cup," Jesse had boasted – and Andy Higgins, who had moved to

Tamarack from another town, had played two years of atom lacrosse before he turned peewee age.

In a surprisingly short period, the Screech Owls peewee hockey team, one of the best peewee hockey teams around, became a passable lacrosse team. So much of the winter game translated perfectly to the summer game, and the differences, for the most part, were obvious. Concrete instead of ice. Sneakers instead of skates. A stick with a pocket for catching and carrying the ball instead of a stick with a curved blade for taking passes and shooting a puck. Yet so many of the passing and checking patterns remained the same. And the idea of both games was exactly the same: put the round object in the other team's net more often than they can put it in yours.

"Goaltenders are a big difference," Muck explained at the Owls' second practice. "More goals are scored in lacrosse. Lots more goals."

"*Yes!*" shouted Nish, who lived to score goals.

"And the goalie has no protection," said Muck. "Once he leaves his crease, he's fair game."

"*Yes!*" shouted Nish, who was forever picking up penalties for "accidentally" running over goalies.

"Now, we need a very, very special player for this position," Muck continued. "We need someone who's big – someone with a great big butt that's going to fill our net so there's no room for anything else to get in."

"*Yes!*" shouted Sarah and Sam, both of them pointing at the only Screech Owl who could possibly fill Muck's requirements.

"*No way!*" Nish shouted. "I'm an 'out' player – I don't do goal!"

"You're sure?" Muck asked, both eyebrows arching.

"I *score* goals," Nish protested, his face reddening and twisting. "I don't *stop* goals."

"Well," said Muck, "what if I told you that lacrosse goalies can carry the ball all they like."

"*Who cares?*" Nish whined.

"What if I told you that lacrosse goalies can cross centre, unlike hockey goalies, and that they can even try to score if they have a chance."

"*Big deal,*" Nish groaned.

"What if I told you that, in lacrosse, the goalie is the glory position?"

Nish's big face twisted so tight it seemed to Travis it might soon start dripping water. No one said a word. Nish opened his mouth as if to speak, then closed it again as if suddenly unsure.

Muck waited patiently, flicking the new white lacrosse ball up and down in his stick pocket and staring at Nish, a small smile on his face.

Nish twisted and sputtered and finally gave in. "I'll think about it."

Nish turned out to be a wonderful goaltender. With his double chest pad on, his big shoulder pads and pants, his flopping shin pads, and his heavy helmet and cage, he seemed two or three times larger than when he was dressed for hockey. He was large, but also quick, and he took so easily to the game that even Muck appeared surprised.

Travis knew for certain it was Nish deep inside all that padding when, during a scrimmage, Nish blocked a shot and scooped it up in the big, wide goalie stick and headed straight up the floor towards the far net.

At the far end, Jeremy Weathers was still trying to get used to the thicker, heavier equipment of the lacrosse goaltender. Only little Simon Milliken was back, and Nish used his weight and bulky equipment to run right over him as if he were a pile of earth and Nish a bulldozer. He came in, faked once, and ripped a hard sidearm shot that clicked in off the far post behind Jeremy.

Anyone else would have turned and trotted back down the floor, but not Nish. He dove into Jeremy's net, knocking the smaller goaltender aside, and grabbed the still-bouncing India rubber ball. Once he had it, he wiggled back out and, holding the ball over his head as if it were the Stanley Cup, raced around the rink boards, tipping his helmet at an imaginary, cheering crowd.

Nish had found his natural position.

4

TRAVIS LOVED LACROSSE. IT TOOK A WHILE TO get used to the new equipment – the thick pads over his lower back, the loose gloves – but nearly half of what he wore was from his hockey bag: the same helmet, the same shoulder pads with a plastic extension tied on to give his arms more protection, the same elbow pads, even the same Screech Owls sweater, which he continued to kiss for good luck as he pulled it over his head.

The stick was another matter. Tamarack Sports had brought in a shipment of Brines – wooden shafts, plastic heads, and nylon braid pockets – and all the Owls had been outfitted with them, each shaft carefully cut to length by Mr. Dillinger. Unlike in hockey, sticks in lacrosse were expected to last several seasons, not a few games.

Travis's new stick had a nice weight, but at first it seemed awkward in his hands. He could scoop up the ball so it skipped into the pocket, but as soon as he tried any of the fancy twirls or fakes that Jesse was so good at, the ball would drop or go flying off in the wrong direction.

But he kept working at it, sometimes alone against the back wall of the house – the steady thumping almost driving his parents crazy – sometimes against the wall of the school gymnasium, and more often than not, now that they were best friends again, out in the street with Nish.

Nish had shown up the very next morning after *The Blood Children: Part VIII*, behaving as if nothing at all had happened. The way Nish acted, he and Travis might have been to see the latest Walt Disney with a church group, after which they'd had a pleasant discussion and then walked home to say their prayers before bed. Not a word about the spilled Sprite, or the fight, or the two of them getting banned for life from the Bluebird Theatre by Mr. Dinsmore.

Travis found he could not say anything about the graveyard. By the time he'd made it home that night, his heart was back in his chest and his brain was refusing to accept what he had seen. Mr. and Mrs. Lindsay had still been up when he arrived home. They had no idea what movie the two boys had gone to see. Travis's mother had put out chewy chocolate chip cookies for him, and he found a cold root beer in the refrigerator. By the time he had started on his third cookie he'd convinced himself there had been no boy and no light and no one crying and no reason whatsoever to think that anything had happened as he passed by the graveyard. It was all his imagination, triggered by the horror movie, the shadows, and the wind.

By morning, when his mother tapped on his bedroom door to let him know that Nish was outside, waiting for him, he'd practically forgotten about it.

They'd tossed the ball around a bit in the yard, then walked up Church Street towards the school, where Nish began to chalk out a net on the brick wall of the gym.

Travis knew he was starting to get a feel for the game. While Nish worked on the net, Travis fired the ball again and again against the wall, the solid *thump . . . thump . . . thump* so comforting in its steady repetition. He loved the way the India rubber ball smacked against the brick wall, seeming to bounce back faster than it had flown into it, and whispered to a stop in the leather cushion of his stick.

Whip . . . smack . . . hiss . . .
Whip . . . smack . . . hiss . . .

Nish had almost finished drawing his net. It seemed small to Travis. He knew that the net was not as wide in lacrosse as in hockey, but this seemed narrower still, and not nearly as tall as it should be.

Nish was, of course, giving himself every possible advantage. He stepped back, considering his art.

"You know what I've decided?" Nish asked, not even looking towards Travis.

Travis caught the ball and held, his rhythm broken, and waited for Nish to continue. "What?" he prodded.

Nish stared at the wall, almost as if he hadn't yet decided anything.

"I don't think *The Blood Children: Part VIII* was a very good movie."

"How would you know?" Travis asked. "You never even saw it."

"I saw enough to know it sucked," Nish said, as if he was the world's number-one movie critic.

"It wasn't bad," argued Travis, who still resented not seeing the ending.

"It wasn't scary at all," Nish said.

Travis said nothing. He couldn't tell Nish about the boy and the graveyard. Nish would not only laugh at him, he'd tell everybody in town.

"I could do better than that myself," Nish continued.

Travis dropped the ball out of his stick. "What's that supposed to mean?"

"I'm gonna make my own horror flick, that's what."

5

TRAVIS OFTEN WONDERED WHERE NISH GOT HIS ideas. Was there a closet somewhere in the Nishikawa home that held every stupid, ridiculous, impossible thought every twelve-year-old kid had ever dared think?

No, Travis thought, it wouldn't be a closet. It would have to be a toilet.

But what amazed Travis most was Nish's ability to get other people caught up in his dumb schemes. Even people with common sense, like Data, who'd figured out how to get Nish's bare butt up on the big Times Square television screen at New Year's.

The horror-flick idea proved even more popular than most.

Fahd, of course, had the camera. Simon and Sarah thought they could write a script. Data could edit the movie on his computer. Everyone – even Travis, he finally had to admit to himself – wanted to play a part in it. Any part at all.

Nish couldn't decide whether he wanted to direct or be the star – and finally settled it by saying he would do both.

"That's not fair," Sam had protested.

"Lots of big stars direct themselves," Nish had said. "Sylvester Stallone, Clint Eastwood."

Fahd and Data, who knew a lot more about movies than Nish did, said the whole idea wasn't nearly as far-fetched as some of the others thought. Fahd knew about all sorts of cheap productions that had gone on to huge success. "*The Blair Witch Project* was a horror movie made by a bunch of students," he told them. "It cost sixty thousand dollars to make and pulled in 140 million – so it's not impossible."

Nish instantly decided that 140 million dollars would be the *minimum* they would make with their movie. A movie that, at the moment, had one used camera, no script, no plot – not even a title.

No matter, Nish was already spending his millions. A new bus for the Screech Owls, of course, with complete stereo and video controls at every plush leather seat. Perhaps even a team plane to take them around the world. "I want to play in Australia," he said, "and in China and in Africa and, for my good buddy, Wilson, in Jamaica."

Wilson laughed. "There's no rinks in Jamaica."

"So?" Nish asked with a shrug. "I'll build one."

"Shouldn't you think about the movie first?" Sam asked. "You're spending the profits and you don't even know what the movie's going to be about."

"I have *people* to do that," Nish said, with a

wave of the hand towards the rest of the Owls.

And so the debate began. They gathered around a picnic table in the park, and for more than an hour talked about possible plots.

Simon and Fahd wanted to make a movie about aliens who land in Tamarack but make the mistake of dropping their flying saucer through the arena roof in the midst of a Screech Owls hockey game and are sliced to tiny, bloody bits by the skates of the hockey players.

"Stupid," said Nish.

Andy wanted to make a vampire film, with plenty of blood-sucking and graveyard scenes and open caskets and people walking around town with garlic bulbs hanging around their necks.

"Can't stand garlic," Nish decided.

"Frankenstein!" Jenny shouted. "Someone builds a monster in science class and it wakes up at night and terrorizes the town."

"Been done too many times," said Nish.

"The flesh-eating Windigo!" Jesse offered. "It comes out on snowy nights and scares people half to death."

"Where would we get snow?" Nish asked.

"Good point," Jesse said, disheartened.

They talked about invasions of deadly bacteria, about how they'd stage exploding bodies, about how they'd film spaceships. Every suggestion seemed to have a huge strike against it. Too expensive. Too difficult. Too corny. Too *un*-scary.

Nish slammed his meaty hand down on the picnic table. "We need something original. A story no one has ever done before."

Travis found himself speaking even before he knew what he was saying. He couldn't believe it. Here he was, the one who knew best how impossible Nish's schemes could be, the one who had seen a thousand Nish brainstorms wash out in their execution.

"There is one," he said, quietly.

A silence fell around the picnic table. Travis could almost hear the heads turning towards him, the eyes all waiting.

"And that is . . . ?" Sarah prodded.

"Tamarack has its own horror story," Travis said, "only I'm not that sure about it."

"What do you mean, not sure about it?" Sam asked.

"I just remember my grandfather and one of his friends once discussing something terrible that happened out on the River Road – something really awful that my grandfather said was the worst thing that ever happened here."

"Well," Nish said impatiently, "*what was it?*"

"I don't know. They stopped talking about it when I came in the room."

"Well," Sam said, "*find out*."

28

6

IT WAS THE DAY OF THE SCREECH OWLS' FIRST lacrosse game ever. They were scheduled to play the Toronto Mini-Rock, a peewee version of the Toronto Rock professional lacrosse team, with identical sweaters, their own team bus – and an *attitude*.

Some of the Owls had gone over to the rink that morning to catch the arrival of the Toronto team. They seemed, to the Owls, much bigger, much older, and much more arrogant than their own little team. They got off the bus with a cocky, know-it-all swagger, all decked out in team sweats with the Rock logo, and all with equipment bags that looked so professional Travis was glad none of the Owls had bothered to cart along their own equipment.

Several of the Mini-Rock players took out their sticks – each one a brand-new, top-of-the-line Brine with the loose strings carefully braided – and they whipped the ball around so quickly Travis could hardly follow it.

They never missed a pass. The ball never struck the sides of their sticks. The Mini-Rock players whipped back passes and underarm passes and sidearm passes. They even played a game in which the player making the catch had to hold his stick up perfectly steady, without moving it no matter what the throw, and each time the ball flew directly in without so much as a tick against the side.

"I think I just came down with an injury," Nish said.

"Me, too," said Andy.

Muck held a brief warm-up practice shortly after noon. To give them a feel for the upcoming game, Muck had the Owls simply run in two different circles, the players in each circle lobbing the ball between each other. They took a few shots at Nish – none of which he stopped – and then Muck sent them out on laps while he headed off in the direction of the coach's dressing room.

"What's with Muck?" Nish shouted at Travis as he puffed up from behind him.

"Looks like he's quitting!" shouted Fahd from the other side.

"Muck doesn't quit," said Travis.

They ran until they could feel the sweat rolling out of their helmets and all the way down to the small of their backs. They ran until the balls of their feet stung. They ran, and ran, until the rink filled with a sound far more familiar from winter: Muck's whistle.

Muck was in the home players' box, and he was no longer alone. Standing at his side was a very old man with white, white hair and the thickest glasses Travis had ever seen. It looked as if he was staring out at the Owls through those little shot glasses Mr. Lindsay kept in the locked liquor cabinet.

The Screech Owls looped over towards the players' bench and the cool relief of the water bottles. Most didn't even bother to drink, just tilted their masks back on their heads, grabbed the plastic bottles, raised them high, and sprayed.

Lacrosse sweat, Travis decided, was different from hockey sweat. Twice as much and twice as warm. It always amazed him how, in a hockey game, a good sweat could almost cool him at the end of a hard shift. Not so in this game. This sweat was like scalding water on the skin. *Salted* scalding water.

Muck opened the door and stepped aside for the old man to step out onto the floor.

Travis could hardly believe what he was seeing through his stinging, blinking, sweat-filled eyes.

The old man had sneakers on. And white shorts with green stripes identical to Muck's. And he was carrying a lacrosse stick unlike any other on the floor.

The old man's stick was made from a single piece of wood, and wood so polished from use, the shaft seemed to shine in his hands. It curved at the end like a shepherd's crook, and the loop was completed by something that looked like hard leather. The pocket itself was leather while the pockets of the kids' sticks were nylon string. And the loose leather strands at the end of his stick were perfectly braided and each one tied off with a different colour of bright cloth.

Travis had never seen such a stick before. It was . . . well . . . *beautiful*, but he couldn't see how it would be good for anything, unless you hung it on a rec-room wall and called it an antique.

Muck cleared his throat, a signal for them all to pay careful attention. "This is Mr. Fontaine," he said.

"Hello, boys," Mr. Fontaine said.

How bad are his eyes? Travis wondered. Can't he see there are girls on this team?

"And girls," Sam corrected.

Mr. Fontaine blinked, looked around several times. "Yes, yes," he said. "Sorry about that. Muck told me there were girls on this team – something we sure didn't have in our day."

"Mr. Fontaine was my coach when I played lacrosse," said Muck. "He knows more about this game than anyone standing here knows about hockey – so listen to everything he says. He'll be working with us this summer."

Travis couldn't help looking over at Nish, who was rolling his eyes. Nish usually didn't have time for anyone even a few years older than he was, let alone several decades. And he was a firm believer in modern equipment – the best new skates, the best pants, top-of-the-line sneakers, the right logo on his T-shirt and baseball cap, the tiniest cellphone, the number-one video game, CD, or movie.

There was only one kind of antique Nish liked, he once told Travis. Leftovers in the refrigerator!

Muck picked up his whistle and blew it lightly. "Let's work on some drills."

Travis had been working at the far end of the floor with Sarah and Dmitri – Muck was keeping them to their hockey lines for the time being – and he was trying to get around Sam and Fahd for a clean shot on Nish.

His size was hurting him. In hockey he had his speed to take him around defence, but in lacrosse you either went right through the defence or else you tucked the ball in tight to your body and tried to roll through. Cross-checking was perfectly legal in lacrosse, and Sam, with her great strength, was almost flicking Travis away like a pesky mosquito every time he tried to break through for a shot.

"You're having trouble, eh, son?" Mr. Fontaine said, noting the obvious.

"I guess," Travis said.

"You know," Mr. Fontaine continued, "it's not necessary for you and the ball to travel together –

so long as you both reach your destination at the same time."

Travis had no idea what the old man meant.

Mr. Fontaine took the ball from Travis and dropped it into his own old stick. It made absolutely no sound as it fell, cradled deep inside the leather.

Mr. Fontaine moved the stick to his shoulder, then whipped it hard in a shot aimed straight at Nish's head. Nish hit the concrete – but the ball was still in Mr. Fontaine's stick!

"You okay, son?" the old man called to Nish. "Slip on something?"

Nish mumbled something in response and scrambled back to his feet.

The rest of the Owls had gathered to watch. Those who had seen the fake were in shock. They had never seen a stick move so quickly, almost like a frog's tongue flicking a passing fly out of mid-air.

"Now," Mr. Fontaine said to Sam, "you try to stop me – okay?"

Sam seemed unsure. "O-kay," she said.

The old man looked at her hard. "I mean *stop* me, understand?"

Sam still seemed uncertain. "I guess," she said.

The old man flicked a few fakes. It seemed, to Travis, as if he were playing with a huge Yo-Yo instead of a lacrosse stick. Once, he even turned the stick upside-down and swung it in a perfect

360-degree circle, handing it off behind his back, and *still* the ball held its position snug in the pocket.

The old man began running at Sam. Travis had never seen such skinny, blue-veined legs. They were white as the lacrosse ball. And they also seemed unsteady, as if he shouldn't even be walking, let alone running on an arena floor.

Sam was red with embarrassment for the old man. She made a half-hearted effort. Mr. Fontaine snapped out a fake that sent her screaming to the floor, convinced he had just sliced her ear off.

The old man flicked his stick so that it lobbed the ball slowly back and over his head, then without looking he stabbed the stick behind his back, catching the ball again perfectly. He seemed to know, instinctively, where the ball would be.

Mr. Fontaine helped Sam up.

"I mean *stop* me, my dear, don't pity me."

"Y-y-yes, sir," Sam said.

He circled back, bouncing the ball and picking it up again without so much as a glance as he turned on those spindly, weak legs and charged again.

This time Sam came out hard, her stick held up to block the old man.

He faked ever so gently with one shoulder. Sam spread her feet, prepared for any turn he might take.

Quick as a snap, Mr. Fontaine bounced the ball between her legs as she turned to go the other way with him. He slipped around the other side, caught the ball on its way up, faked once to put Nish into a sliding block, and then whipped the stick around his back to drop an unbelievable backhander into the net.

"*My God!*" Andy said beside Travis.

"*Unbelievable!*" added Jesse.

Mr. Fontaine reached into the net, spun his stick effortlessly against the ball as it rolled about the concrete floor, and pulled his stick away with the ball once again nestled perfectly in the pocket.

I would die happy, Travis thought, if only once I could pick up the ball like that.

The old man came trotting back to Travis. He held out his stick, turned it over, and deposited the ball in Travis's hand.

"Now you try it," he said.

7

FOUR HOURS LATER, THE SCREECH OWLS WERE losing 17–5 to the Toronto Mini-Rock. The score was hardly unexpected; they were only just beginning and the Toronto team had been around for years. What was important, Muck told them, was not who won, but how the Screech Owls developed as a team. The game would give them a sense of how far they had yet to go before they could call themselves a lacrosse team.

Nish had played well. He had blocked dozens of shots, some of them while lying on his stomach in his crease and kicking up his legs. Balls had hit him on the head, on the chest, on his toes, and once even on his butt when he got so confused he forgot which way he was facing.

Sarah, too, had played well, though she was up against a huge centre who at first kept bowling her over whenever they fought for a loose ball. Her opponent was the Mini-Rock's top player, but she didn't let him overwhelm her. Her play-making skills in hockey were all evident in lacrosse, and she had good enough speed to keep up with and even beat the Mini-Rock forwards.

She had scored three of the Owls' goals, and twice sent Dmitri in on breakaways. Dmitri was easily the fastest player on the floor, but he kept dropping the ball before he could get a shot away.

Travis had his own troubles. He kept getting knocked away from the play. He couldn't win the corners, and he couldn't break through the defence to give Sarah another target apart from Dmitri.

Late in the third Sarah cleanly won a draw and broke up-floor quickly. She threw the ball to Dmitri, who caught it and began racing down the far boards.

A large Mini-Rock defenceman came out and drilled him with a hard cross-check, spilling the ball along the boards, bouncing crazily from sidespin.

Sarah moved past her check and scooped the ball on the run. She set along the far boards, faked a pass to Sam on defence, then threw completely cross-floor to Travis.

Travis felt the ball rattle against his pocket, but it stayed. It felt heavy. He was panicking, and he couldn't stop it. The other defender was charging right at him, stick held out like he was coming to take Travis's head off.

His first instinct was to duck, but he knew that would only make the situation worse.

He stepped towards the defenceman, faked, and the defender stopped, setting. Travis dropped his shoulder, forcing the defender to spread his feet. He bounced the ball through and darted quickly by the surprised defenceman just in time to lunge ahead and catch the ball, barely, before it spun off into the corner.

There was only the goaltender between Travis and the net. The goaltender puffed out his chest pad and came at him. Travis faked again and raced towards the corner, breaking the goalie's angle.

He fired blind. All he saw was the red light flash. All he heard was Sarah's scream.

"YYYYYYYYEEESSSSSSS!"

He had scored the first lacrosse goal of his life – and on Mr. Fontaine's magic play!

Travis loved the feel of his linemates piling on. It had been a meaningless goal – no way could they win – but it had been a beautiful one.

At the bench even Muck was smiling. Travis came off, and Data tossed a towel around his neck as he took his seat on the bench.

Travis felt a pair of hands on his shoulders. They were the oldest-looking hands he had ever seen. Pure white where they weren't freckled or liver-spotted. Gnarled, bony fingers. Huge, swollen knuckles. They looked as if they might shatter if someone squeezed them. But then *they* squeezed – quickly, and with surprising strength.

And then they were gone.

8

THE FINAL SCORE WAS 19–8 FOR THE TORONTO Mini-Rock. It had been a clean game, and the two teams shook hands. Mr. Dillinger had ice-cold Cokes waiting for them in the dressing room, and Muck took the unusual step of making a very short post-game speech.

"By the end of the season we'll be even with them," Muck said. "Just wait and see."

Travis doubted it, but he still felt very good. Lacrosse was fun, almost as much fun as hockey, and he had to wonder if he'd ever scored a sweeter goal in winter than the one he'd scored just now.

"Where's Mr. Fontaine?" Travis asked as the dressing room emptied.

"He never came in," said Derek.

"Went straight from the bench to the front door," said Sam.

Travis shrugged. Perhaps he had to be some-where. Too bad, though, because Travis had wanted to thank him for the lesson.

He drove home with his parents. Mr. Lindsay, who had played a little lacrosse when he was growing up, was delighted with the game and said he hoped this signalled the return of a sport that had simply faded away for lack of interest.

"Who was the old man on the bench with Muck?" Mr. Lindsay asked after a while.

"Mr. Fontaine," Travis said.

"Zeke Fontaine?" Mr. Lindsay asked.

Zeke? Travis wondered. What kind of name is that?

"Just Mr. Fontaine," he said from the back seat. "That's what Muck called him. He's going to help Muck coach."

They drove in silence after that. Mr. Lindsay seemed to be thinking about something else.

Finally, Mrs. Lindsay asked her husband, "Do you know him?"

"I don't know if it's who I think it is," said Mr. Lindsay.

"And who do you think it is?" Mr. Lindsay asked.

"I'd rather not say until I know for sure."

Nish was at Travis's door early the next morning. He'd already forgotten about the loss to the Toronto Mini-Rock and had turned his attention completely to the horror movie that was going to make them millions and show Mr. Dinsmore down at the Bluebird Theatre that he had made a terrible mistake kicking out next year's Oscar winners.

"If we can't find anything local to do it on," Nish was saying, as he helped himself to a huge bowl of Froot Loops and poured on maple syrup instead of milk, "don't worry about it. Fahd and I have been kicking around a few new ideas."

"Like what?" Travis said, busy buttering his toast.

Nish stopped chewing long enough to explain. "Fahd's got this great idea of a humungous ball of gas coming out of space and crashing into Earth and killing everybody. He wants to call it *Fart Wars*."

"Sounds stupid to me," said Travis as he reached for the raspberry jam.

"Me too," Nish said, Froot Loops exploding from his mouth as he talked. "I mean, you can't even *see* a fart. You can't scare anybody unless you can show something that stinks so bad people fall over dead from it."

Travis couldn't resist. "Make the movie about your hockey bag – or better yet, your lacrosse bag. Just unzip it on Main Street and watch people drop like flies!"

"*Very* funny."

"I thought it was."

They set off early to see Travis's grandfather. He and Travis's grandmother lived in the lower part of town where the river widened slightly and Lookout Hill cut off the morning sun.

Old Mr. Lindsay, a retired policeman, had lived

his entire life in Tamarack. His father had been a logger in the days when the magnificent white pine in the hills around town had been shipped all over the world. His grandfather had been a trapper and had built the first cabin ever on the banks of the river. Travis sometimes thought the town should have been named after his family, not after an old tree that grew only in swamps and couldn't hang onto its needles.

They found old Mr. Lindsay in his garage workshop, puttering. His workbench was covered in the old alarm clocks and radios and toasters – pickings from the garbage, favours for neighbours – that he loved to spend his spare time figuring out and fixing. There was a cup of coffee steaming beside the vise and, hanging off the edge of the workbench, a large smouldering Corona cigar sending smoke twisting towards the fluorescent light. Old Mr. Lindsay was not allowed to smoke in the house, which made Travis wonder if he really enjoyed fixing the neighbours' broken appliances or whether he simply needed an excuse to get out of the house and light up.

"Good mornin', boys," the old man said as he set down his glasses and reached for his coffee. "Radio says you came up short last night. Sorry I couldn't make the game."

"You didn't miss much," said Nish.

"Said on the radio you scored one, Trav. Good on you. What about you, Mr. Nishikawa? Pretty unusual for you to be kept off the scoresheet."

"I'm playing goal," Nish muttered. "Biggest mistake I ever made in my life."

Old Mr. Lindsay stared at Nish a moment, his eyes twinkling and a little smile growing. "I doubt that – I doubt that very much."

A small radio lay in pieces before the old man. He was checking the circuits with a tiny screwdriver that had a light bulb at the end which flashed whenever he touched a live wire. He put his glasses back on and returned to the task at hand, well used to having the two boys drop in and watch.

Nish nudged Travis with his elbow.

"Grandpa . . . ?" Travis began.

"Yes, sir?" the old man answered without looking up.

"What's the *worst* thing that ever happened in Tamarack?"

"That new traffic light on Church and Main. Why?"

"No, I mean a long, long time ago – back when you were young."

The old man looked up and grinned. He tilted his glasses onto the top of his head. Travis now had his full attention.

"Well, that would have to be the meteor that killed off all the dinosaurs, wouldn't it?"

Travis shook his head. He liked his grandfather's strange sense of humour, even if he rarely got the joke.

"No, when you were a cop – a policeman, I mean."

"You mean a cop. That's what we called ourselves, and nothing wrong with it, either."

The old man paused, sipped his coffee, and picked up the smouldering cigar and shoved it into his mouth. "I handled a murder investigation all by myself once," he finally said, puffing on the cigar, his eyes almost closed. "But that was two crazy drunken brothers arguing about whose turn it was to go out to the woodpile. It wasn't a nice thing, but hardly the worst."

"What about that thing out on River Road you and Mr. Donahue were talking about one day when I was over?"

The cigar came out and old Mr. Lindsay set it down, hard. He was no longer smiling. He pushed his glasses back into place on his nose, and turned back to his work.

"I don't remember," he said.

Travis was taken aback. His grandfather suddenly seemed so cold and uninterested. Perhaps he really didn't remember. Travis's grandmother was always going on about how his grandfather could lose his glasses on the top of his head, and how he had to write down everything he intended to do each day – and then usually lost the note.

"River Road," Travis repeated. "Something about –"

But Travis's grandfather cut him off with a curt "*No.*" End of topic. No further discussion.

They stayed around and watched the old man work, but there was hardly any more talk. Travis's grandfather seemed almost in another world, and they were not going to be invited in. After a while they said they had to go and together they walked down towards the river wondering what they could do now.

"Far as I'm concerned," said Nish, "I'm more curious than ever to know what the story is."

"So am I," said Travis.

"You got any ideas?"

Travis didn't. They could search through the library files to see what the local newspaper might have written, but they didn't even know what the topic was. Besides, a little newspaper whose front page featured ribbon-cutting ceremonies wasn't likely to contain a story that even the police wouldn't discuss.

"What about this Mr. Donahue you mentioned?" asked Nish.

"He's in the retirement home," Travis said. "My grandparents go and visit him sometimes, but Grandma says it's hardly worthwhile. He lives in the past."

Nish turned and stared at Travis, his eyes growing wide. "Well?" he said. "Could we ask for anything better than that?"

（

9

AUTUMN LEAVES RETIREMENT HOME LAY JUST
beyond the arena on the bank of the river where
a small rapids ran along one side of the waterway
and a large, deep pool lay along the other. Across
the water, the sidewalks and lights of River Street
came to an end and River Road, a gravel road
now heavily oiled to keep down the dust, began.
Beyond that lay the marina, the town dump, a
few farms, the lake, and the seemingly never-
ending bush.

It wasn't Travis's first time at the home. He'd
come with his parents to visit a great-aunt who
had died a year earlier. Nish, however, had never
been, and didn't have a clue how to behave once
he got there.

"Where do you think *you're* going, young
man?" a turtle-faced woman demanded as he
sauntered past the reception desk without so
much as a nod in her direction.

"To see Mr. Donahue," Nish answered, barely
breaking stride.

"You'll have to sign in," she snapped.

47

Nish stopped, heading to the visitors' book and grabbing for the pen that dangled off the end of a string attached to the desk.

"Are you family?" she demanded.

"That's right," Nish answered.

She stared at him over the tops of her glasses. Travis could hardly blame her; Nish looked as likely a relative of old Mr. Donahue as the retirement home looked like the hockey rink.

Nish never missed a beat. Catching her suspicion before it had time to go anywhere, he turned and pointed at Travis. "*He* is."

"I see," said the turtle. "What family, exactly?"

Travis had to think fast. "Nephew," he said. It wasn't exactly a lie; there had been a time when he was told to call Mr. Donahue "Uncle Ralph" because Travis's grandfather and the old man were best friends together on the police force.

The turtle looked dubious, but let them pass after they'd signed in.

"He's in 228," she shouted after them.

They found the room at the far end of the second floor, but getting there was a bit unnerving. An old man in a wheelchair had been singing songs without words as they passed. An old woman, her stockings fallen down around her ankles, had sworn at them and swung at Nish with her cane.

"Remind me not to get old," Nish whispered

behind his hand as they headed down the corridor.

Travis said nothing. He felt sorry for these people and was glad that his own grandparents were still healthy and living in their own house. He tried to imagine Nish as an old man living here, but couldn't. Would he be mooning everyone who passed? Would he be wearing X-ray glasses to see through the nurses' uniforms? Would he lie in bed screaming "I'M GONNA HURL!" every time a doctor came close?

They knocked at the partially open door.

"*Get in out of the rain!*" an old voice cried out from the other side.

Nish turned to Travis and made a face. Was that a joke? Or did the person inside really think it was raining in the hallway?

Travis recognized Mr. Donahue at once. He was sitting in a chair beside his bed and was just pushing away his food tray after the noon meal. He was completely bald, his head as polished as the top of the cane Travis's grandmother sometimes used. Mr. Donahue was fully dressed, wearing a tie and navy blazer with a police crest on the breast pocket, but his shirt seemed to belong to someone twice his size. The collar looked like two or three of Mr. Donahue's birdlike neck could have fit inside it.

It was almost as if he had shrunk since Travis had last seen his grandfather's old police friend. Travis couldn't remember how long ago that had been, but at this rate, he thought, in another couple of years Mr. Donahue's neck could fit through one of his blazer buttonholes.

"*Mr. Lindsay!*" the old man shouted. "How kind of you to come."

Travis was amazed the old man remembered him. It took a couple of minutes before he realized Mr. Donahue had not recognized Travis at all. He had mistaken him for his father.

It was soon clear that Mr. Donahue was about thirty years behind the real world. He was still a policeman in his mind. He was talking with his partner's young boy.

Nish understood this faster than Travis. And instead of trying to correct the old man, he let the conversation proceed as if they really were more than thirty years in the past.

Mr. Donahue complained about draft dodgers. He bragged about the Montreal Canadiens – who did he think was playing for them, Travis wondered, Jean Béliveau? And he complained about the boring lunches his wife was packing for him. Travis had never even known there *was* a Mrs. Donahue.

"What's the biggest crime you ever solved?" Nish suddenly asked.

Mr. Donahue looked up, surprised. His pale blue eyes were astonishingly clear, the whites as pure as snow.

"Biggest crime I was ever involved in," he

almost shouted, "was *never* solved — and you two boys know that as well as I know myself."

Travis took a gamble. "River Road," he said mildly.

"*Exactly!*" Mr. Donahue said, shaking a long finger in Travis's direction. "Most terrifying thing I've ever seen in my life."

Nish took a much larger gamble. "What happened?"

Mr. Donahue looked down again. At first the boys wondered if he'd heard. Then they wondered if he'd drifted off to sleep on them. When he finally looked up, the eyes had reddened, and the pale blue glistened under the ceiling lights.

"I don't know, boys. Only one person can answer that question, as far as I'm concerned."

"Who's that?" Nish asked.

Old Mr. Donahue hammered his fist in fury on the arm of his chair. It glanced off and struck the food tray, sending it clattering to the floor.

"*Fontaine!*" he shouted. "*Zeke Fontaine!*"

Travis swallowed hard. He had heard this name only the night before, when his father mentioned it on the way home from the lacrosse game. "Zeke" had sounded funny. Now it struck terror in him.

Sweat had broken out on Nish's forehead. He was leaning towards Mr. Donahue, working so hard to get him to talk that he didn't even see the shadow looming in the doorway and the face of the turtle appear, looking like it was about to bite the handle off a rake.

"*What* is going on in here?" she demanded.

Travis was already picking up the spilled tray. "Nothing – he just dropped his tray, that's all."

"What was all the shouting for?" she snapped. "There's to be *no* shouting at Autumn Leaves."

"*I'll shout when I damn well feel like shouting!*" Mr. Donahue bellowed. Travis realized there was no love lost between the turtle and Mr. Donahue.

"Who are these young men, Mr. Donahue?" she asked.

"I have no idea!" Mr. Donahue snapped back.

"He's one of my grandfather's closest friends," Travis tried to explain as the turtle pushed the two boys towards the front door. He was surprised she didn't twist their ears to hustle them out. "I've known him all my life!"

"Well," the turtle said when they got to the door, "he doesn't know you any more. He doesn't even know who *he* is any more."

With that, she shoved them through the revolving doors and out onto the front steps of Autumn Leaves.

"Who the hell is Zeke Fontaine?" Nish asked as they headed down the driveway towards the river.

"I think I know," said Travis.

"Well," Nish demanded, "*who?*"

"Our lacrosse coach."

10

"ZEKE FONTAINE . . . ," MR. LINDSAY SAID. "I thought he had died years ago."

Travis had gone to the source of the coach's strange first name, and Mr. Lindsay had at last seemed willing to talk about the mysterious old man, even if, as he said, neither he nor anyone else knew the whole story.

"Zeke Fontaine was once a great lacrosse star," Mr. Lindsay said. "Played out west on a couple of Mann Cup teams, I think. He came here in the 1960s and set up the town's minor lacrosse system. At one point lacrosse was as big as hockey around here, you know, but it eventually faded and then vanished altogether – at least until this year, when Muck came along and revived it."

Mr. Lindsay sipped at his coffee and stared out the window. "I should have seen the connection right away," he said, almost to himself.

"What connection?" asked Travis.

"Muck Munro. He was a heck of a hockey player," his father said. "You know that. Probably would have played in the NHL if he hadn't got hurt. But he was an even more talented lacrosse player.

"Zeke Fontaine had two young stars," he continued, "Muck and his own son, Liam. Liam was probably better than Muck. In less than three years Zeke built his team into a national contender. Hadn't lost a single game all year when the bad stuff happened . . ."

"What bad stuff?"

"Liam got killed. At least people *think* Liam got killed – they never found the body. The lacrosse team was headed for the provincial championships, but they never played another game. And Zeke Fontaine never coached another game."

Travis's father was speaking almost dreamily now, as if Travis wasn't even there. He would take his time – Travis knew his father well – but he would tell whatever he knew. Travis would just have to sit. Patiently.

"Zeke Fontaine claimed his son was attacked by a rogue bear. They lived out River Road – I guess he still lives out there – and the old man said his son was walking home from the rink when he got attacked.

"It made some sense. Farmers had been complaining about this huge black bear with a streak of white along one flank that had been attacking their stock – Silvertip, they called it. Some sheep had been killed and eaten, and even some cattle were slaughtered and, I think, a horse. It was pretty ugly.

"There was a huge hunt for the bear. They

brought in rangers and even a couple of army snipers and killed every black bear they could track down. Soon as they killed them, they cut open their stomachs and analyzed the contents, but they couldn't find any evidence whatsoever that any of them had attacked the boy."

Mr. Lindsay fell silent.

"What about the bear, Silvertip?" Travis asked. "Did they shoot it?"

Mr. Lindsay took a long sip, remembering. "They did. Two local policeman, Darby Fenwick and Constable Rodgers – I forget his first name – cornered it back of Lookout Hill and one of them emptied his service revolver into it. But that wasn't enough to stop Silvertip. He charged them both. Tore them to ribbons. Rodgers was killed straight away, but Fenwick took three days to die. Only time I ever saw your grandfather fall down on his knees and bawl. It was the worst thing that ever happened in this town."

"Did they find the bear?"

"No. Never."

"What about the boy?"

"Never found him, either. And that's when the story turned really ugly.

"One of the other kids on the team claimed that Zeke and Liam had had a big fight at the rink, which was why the boy happened to be walking home that day. It's a long haul out to where they lived, you know.

"Anyway, that got the police looking more closely at Zeke. They found a rifle at the house that had been fired recently. They found old clothes burned in a backyard barrel. They found a shovel with fresh dirt on it. Zeke had an answer for everything: he'd been shooting groundhogs; he'd been burning old oil rags; he'd been working in the garden.

"I know your grandfather, for one, never believed him. The police were convinced he'd done his own son in and sent the police on a wild goose chase – I guess you could say wild *bear* chase – that had cost the force two good men. They blamed Fontaine for their deaths."

"Did they charge him?"

Mr. Lindsay shook his head. "Couldn't. Never found the boy's body. Never had any evidence apart from their own suspicions."

"Wasn't that enough?"

"Never stand up for a minute in court."

"So what happened?"

"Nothing. The town turned against Fontaine. He left town. I thought he moved back to the West Coast, where he'd played. I guess he moved back here after he retired. No one ever bought the Fontaine property even though it was listed for sale – people thought it was cursed after the three deaths, I guess. Only person who stood by Zeke was Muck Munro."

"Muck?"

"Yep. And Muck, you'd think, would have reasons of his own to blame the old man. He'd lost his lacrosse team. He'd lost his chance at the provincial championship. He'd lost his best friend on the team. But unlike practically everyone else in Tamarack, he never once blamed Zeke for what had happened."

"How did Muck get him to coach again?"

"Who knows? Maybe he thinks getting him back in lacrosse will do him good. Maybe he sees in you Owls what the two of them lost after Liam went missing – a chance to win the provincial championship."

"*Our* team? Not very likely."

"You never know," said Mr. Lindsay, finally smiling again. "Who's to say Nish isn't the greatest goaltending prospect in lacrosse history?"

"*Get real*," said Travis.

An hour later the Screech Owls knew all about Liam Fontaine, Silvertip, the two dead policemen, and the great mystery of Zeke Fontaine, their new coach.

"It makes my skin crawl," said Sarah.

"Fantastic," said Nish.

Sarah turned on Nish, appalled. "Why would you say something like *that?*"

"It's *exactly* what we want for our movie!"

11

TRAVIS WAS GETTING A FEEL FOR LACROSSE. THE Owls practised daily – Muck handling the drills, Zeke Fontaine teaching individual skills – and it seemed when they weren't officially practising or working on Nish's crazy horror movie, two or three or more of the Screech Owls were gathering at the school to toss the ball around and try pick-ups and fakes and back passes.

Three games into the season, Sarah had emerged as the team's number-one star, just as she was in hockey. She moved down the floor with the same easy grace that she had always shown on skates. And if she read the game well in hockey, it was nothing compared to how she could read plays in lacrosse: tossing balls to seemingly empty spaces, only to have her passes arrive perfectly on time; finding openings for shots and setting up from behind the opposition net in a way that might have made even Wayne Gretzky applaud.

The oddest thing about Sarah, Travis noticed, was that she made no noise as she ran. Her sneakers barely whispered as they met the floor. No huffing and puffing. Nothing. Like a film without sound. Travis, on the other hand, slapped up and down the concrete. But he was barely audible compared to Nish.

Nish, too, was growing into his role. When he moved, it was like an old train starting up. His sneakers squeaked and screeched and flapped. The foot guards of his big shin pads snapped against the tops of his sneakers. And he grunted with every effort as he moved about in the big, bulky goaltending equipment.

Nish was challenging more, coming out and chasing balls into the corners, then using his good throwing ability to send long breakaway passes down the floor. Dmitri, finally getting a feel for his stick, had become a major scoring threat with his speed, and Nish was starting to look for him more and more. Sam, with her strength, was turning into an excellent defence player, tough, determined, her cross-checks leaving opposing players wincing even before she struck.

Travis was quickly becoming the team's most skilled stickhandler. He found he had the *touch* in lacrosse. He could tell, instinctively, which way and how high a spinning loose ball would bounce. He was able to pick up rolling balls on the run, using a wonderful spin of the pocket over the ball that Mr. Fontaine had taught him.

"This way," the old man had said, "you won't have to run straight at a ball the way players who scoop balls need to. You become like a cat with this move, able to strike from anywhere – even pluck a ball right out of another player's stick."

For whatever reason, Mr. Fontaine had decided Travis was his "project." He told him he was passing on his secrets, and as soon as Travis mastered one of them the other Screech Owls would be demanding he teach it to them after practice.

Mr. Fontaine taught him how to "steal" a ball from a player foolish enough to hold the ball out front as he looked for a play. "You have your pocket upside-down," he said, "and you come down hard on his pocket with your stick, spinning just when the two pockets hit."

It took Travis the better part of a morning to master that one, but eventually he could do it. It happened so fast it reminded Travis of the magician's cup-and-pea trick. There really were things that could happen faster than the eye can see.

"You're good with that stick, boy," the old man said one morning after practice. "But I think you'd be even better with a *real* stick."

By "real" Mr. Fontaine meant "wooden." He said to Travis he thought the Owls' fancy new Brine sticks were flashy but useless. He himself used a very old but perfectly preserved Logan – a legendary lacrosse stick, Muck told them, once made on the Six Nations Reserve in southwestern Ontario. And true enough, it seemed that Mr. Fontaine could fake far better than they ever could, and even shoot harder than any of them, with the possible exception of Sam.

They put it down to experience.

"I want you to try mine," the old man said to Travis one day as practice was breaking up. He handed Travis the Logan; Travis handed him the Brine.

He weighed the old stick in his hands. It felt awkward and unbalanced. It was heavier than his Brine. And it smelled.

Mr. Fontaine noticed Travis sniffing the pocket area. He smiled. "Linseed oil," he said. "Keeps the catgut flexible."

"Catgut?" Travis asked.

"The edge of the pocket opposite the wood," the old man explained. "It's called catgut."

Travis looked hard at the edge. It was yellowed and stringy and hard, but flexible at the same time. Strung together as it was, it formed a "fence" between the soft pocket and the outside of the stick, and allowed a player to keep the ball tucked safely in the pocket. Travis's stick, of course, was hard plastic on both sides.

He was afraid to ask where the catgut came from.

He was, in fact, afraid of Mr. Fontaine. *Terrified* of him. The old man never looked directly at the kids as he talked to them. Perhaps it was just the thick glasses, but the effect was a little creepy. And he never spoke to them all as a group. Always one on one. He didn't learn their last names — a blessing, Travis figured, since he was a Lindsay and the old man might connect it to the policeman who tried to nail him for murder so many years ago — and he didn't hang about after practice the way Muck sometimes did just to talk or throw the ball around for fun.

"Like it?" Mr. Fontaine said after Travis had picked up a few loose balls and tried a few throws with the Logan.

In a way he did; in a way he didn't. He didn't have a feel for it yet, but he could tell, when he threw, that there was a wonderful *power* in the old man's wooden stick. When Travis shot with his Brine, there was no feeling apart from the thrust. When he shot with the Logan, it was as if he could feel every roll of the ball as it came out of the pocket, almost as if, when the ball was released, it got an extra kick from the laces that Mr. Fontaine so carefully worked through the upper portion of the pocket.

"Yeah, sure," Travis said.

"You come out to my place this afternoon. I've got something for you."

Travis looked up. For the first time that he noticed, Mr. Fontaine was looking directly at him. He could see pain in his old eyes — almost as if they were on the verge of tears — and Travis knew that he couldn't say what he so desperately wanted to say. *No, thanks.*

Instead, he said what he felt he *had* to say: "O-kay."

He felt a shiver go down his spine. It was probably the hottest day of summer. He was covered in sweat from the practice. But it still felt as if an icicle had just slid down to the small of his back.

Muck's whistle blew at centre floor. Travis handed the wooden stick back, took his Brine, and ran, feet slapping on the floor, to join the scrum.

Muck had a piece of paper in his hands. "I have here a letter from the Lacrosse Association," he began, before starting to read. "'Dear Mr. Munro . . . etc., etc., etc. . . . We are pleased to announce that your application to have Tamarack host this year's provincial championship for peewee has been accepted. The dates suggested by your committee are also approved, and invitations have been issued this week to fourteen teams.'"

"YYESSSS!" shouted Sarah.

Muck folded the paper and stuck it into the back pocket of his old shorts. "We have a lot of work still to do," he said.

12

THE MOVIEMAKERS HAD A LOT OF WORK TO DO, too. Fahd and Data had organized the cameras – they already had Fahd's video and had borrowed another from Mr. Dillinger – and Data was even helping Sarah work out a plot outline on his laptop computer, but they still needed to know more.

Simon was worried about how they would ever get film of bears around Tamarack.

"There are always bears out at the dump," Jesse said.

"That's hardly what we're looking for," Nish, the Hollywood director, argued. "You're talking about bears ripping apart green garbage bags. I'm looking for bears that rip apart *people!*"

"How are you going to arrange that, Movie Boy?" asked Sarah. "Or are you going to *volunteer?*"

"Very funny," Nish said. "We find the bear – then we worry about how we make it look like it's attacking two policemen. Maybe we use dummies. With a lot of blood and guts and quick cuts, no one will be able to tell the difference."

"There's only one dummy in this movie," Sarah shot back.

The team meeting about the horror movie did not go well. Some of the Owls were beginning to lose interest in Nish's project. Others wanted to abandon the idea of a local story in favour of another crazy idea from Fahd. Fahd wanted to use one camera to film closeups of frogs and toads and salamanders and snakes and spiders, then use the other camera to take shots of downtown Tamarack, and run the two together and call it *Invasion of the Creepy Crawlies*.

"Brilliant," Nish said with all the sarcasm he could muster. "Positively *brilliant*, my dear Fahd."

"Thanks," Fahd said.

"C'mon, Trav," Nish said, scooping up the notes he was making in an unused school exercise book, of which he seemed to have dozens. "We're wasting our time here."

Travis and Nish headed out River Road on their mountain bikes. Both carried their lacrosse sticks carefully tied along the crossbar and hanging out in front. Travis had a ball stuffed deep in his pocket. Nish had his backpack, and in the pack he had Mr. Dillinger's video camera. They were going, Travis had told him, on a "scouting" mission.

"Fontaine invited you out?" Nish had asked Travis.

"Yeah," Travis said. "He said he had something for me."

"Maybe a bullet!" Nish said, giggling.

"That's not funny."

Travis didn't really think he had anything to worry about, going to old man Fontaine's place in the bush, but he was nervous enough not to want to do it alone. He'd convinced Nish to come by saying they'd be able to gain a better sense of setting, and if they took the camera they could stop in at the dump on the way and maybe get some footage of bears.

"Fine with me," said Nish. "Mr. Dillinger's camera has an unbelievable zoom — it'll be like you're close enough to reach out and touch them."

It was now mid-July, the roadside filled with white daisies and orange devil's paintbrushes and yellow buttercups. The farmers along River Road were in the fields, and the air was ripe with the smell of the fresh-cut hay. It was a wonderful day for a bike ride, and Travis only wished he could enjoy it more. His stomach was jumping. He had no idea what Mr. Fontaine wanted him out here for.

They came first to the town dump. It had changed dramatically from when Travis was younger. Sometimes, on a cool summer evening, his family used to drive out to sit in the car and watch the bears pick through the garbage. Occasionally, bear cubs would walk right up to the cars – there might be six or seven bears in all – and sometimes a mother bear would race over and scold her offspring for getting so close.

No cars came out in the evening any more. The dump was fenced off now, and the entrance gate was chained at the end of each day. An attendant was always on hand to ensure that no one dumped toxic materials or paint cans or old tires, and there were recycling bins for everything from glass and plastic to egg cartons and newspapers.

"Still open!" Nish shouted back as he neared the gate.

They pedalled inside and over to the attendant's shed. Travis and Nish both knew the man on duty – an older brother of Ty Barrett, who sometimes helped Muck out with the Owls' hockey practices.

"Looking for 'garbage' goals, boys?" he asked.

"Good one!" Nish said, though Travis could tell he didn't really mean it.

"Any bears?" Travis asked.

"A couple, now and then," the attendant said. "Not like before, though. The ministry came in and shot a few of them this spring, you know. Called them 'nuisance' bears – but who they were bothering is beyond me."

"Damn!" shouted Nish. "We could've filmed that!"

The attendant looked at Nish, waiting for him to explain.

"School project," Nish said. "Trav 'n' me are working on a film about area bears, good or bad."

The attendant lifted his cap and scratched his balding head. "Isn't school out?" he asked.

"This is for next term," Nish explained.

"Would it be all right if we filmed one, if there's one around?" Travis asked.

The attendant took his cap off entirely. His thin wisps of hair were tightly curled and greasy. Travis was struck by how the man's cap left a line that split his face into two distinct parts: one that had seen too much sun, one that had seen no sun at all.

He looked about, almost as if expecting to find a surveillance camera hidden in the pines that bordered the pit where the garbage was thrown.

"Come with me," he said finally.

Nish hauled Mr. Dillinger's camera out of his backpack and the two boys leaned their bikes against the shed as the attendant set off for a far corner of the pit.

Travis's nose felt like it might burst with so many smells, most of them foul and sour. There was only one sound, however, the ill-tempered screeching and calling of hundreds of seagulls. They were everywhere, fighting over the garbage, rising in waves as the attendant kicked a loose green garbage bag down and into the pit, then falling back like a soft blanket of white feathers as the bag settled.

They came to a small stand of pines with cedars growing below. The attendant held his finger to his lips to hush them, then pushed through ahead of the boys.

The branches were in Travis's face. He was hot, and sweating, and the garbage dump stank beyond belief – but then, in an instant, he forgot everything but what he saw before him.

Two black bears were standing over a half-torn garbage bag!

Travis's heart pounded. Sweat dripped down his nose and into the corners of his mouth. A mosquito landed on his cheek and he couldn't even bring himself to slap it for fear of scaring off the two bears.

Scaring them off or, worse, attracting their attention!

Nish was already filming. "Man-oh-man-oh-man," he muttered. "This is just what the director ordered."

Travis worried that Nish might be making too much noise. But the bears seemed to be paying no attention. Travis stared at them, fascinated. At first they seemed smaller than he expected, but then one of them stood on its hind legs and sniffed the air, and Travis knew if he were beside it the animal would tower over him, easily.

The other bear poked his nose at the bag, grunted, and then swiped at it casually with one paw. The paw seemed to move in slow motion, yet despite the lack of effort the bag exploded into a shower of paper and empty containers and plate scrapings.

Travis imagined those same claws hitting a human head. He shuddered.

Nish was filming furiously. "Why-oh-why-oh-why does that have to be a stupid green garbage bag?"

"You'd prefer a body?" the attendant whispered, amused.

"Can you arrange one?" Nish answered.

"Sure," the attendant smiled. "Just walk out there and try to pet one of them."

"*L-look!*" Travis suddenly found himself saying. He pointed beyond the two bears. Up the hill, stopping every now and then to raise a long, pointed nose to test the air, came the largest bear Travis had ever seen. It was at least *twice* the size of the two bears who had just given Travis shivers and shudders with one casual blow of an open paw.

The bear paused, rose onto its haunches, sniffed the air, and turned. It had white hair along the far flank — almost as if someone had spilled bleach along him.

"Silvertip," the attendant said.

Travis's mind raced. *The* Silvertip? Impossible! He would have to be forty or fifty years old.

"Not the one they wanted to kill?" Travis asked.

The attendant shook his head. "Naw. The old guy who works here with me says there was another Silvertip back sometime in the seventies that they hunted but never caught. This one's young – but I still call him Silvertip. Maybe he's a grandson or great-grandson or something. He's a mean beggar anyway. I think maybe we'd be smart to head back."

Travis and Nish didn't need much convincing. The big bear – Silvertip – was now up to the garbage bag the other two bears had been fighting over. The smaller bears had scattered like seagulls on his arrival, both of them scooting back down the bank with their tiny tails between their legs. The boys would have laughed except they had no desire to attract Silvertip's attention.

The big bear stood on his back legs, sniffed, and seemed to stare towards the boys.

Travis's heart stopped. *He's twice as tall as I am!*

But the bear must not have seen them. He half-flicked a paw at a bag and, again, the garbage flew. He buried his head in the trash, grunting and pushing with his nose.

The three spectators backed away through the low cedar.

"Great footage!" Nish kept saying. "*Great* footage!"

But Travis wasn't thinking about movies. They still had one more stop to make on this journey.

71

13

TRAVIS HAD KNOWN THERE WAS A HOUSE OUT here in the deep bush – several times his family had driven this far out River Road to picnic at a nearby widening of the river that everyone in town called "The Lake" – but he had always believed the old place to be abandoned. The entrance was badly overgrown and the old black wood-frame building was barely visible from the gravel road.

There was, however, a mailbox. "B. D. Fo tai e," it read. Both the *n*'s were missing, but Travis had no trouble recognizing the name. Where, he wondered, did they get "Zeke" from?

There was also a sign, worn and fading: "BEWARE OF DOG."

"You're on your own, pal," Nish said as he brought his bike to a gravel-spewing stop. "No way I'm goin' in there."

"I went to see the bears with you," Travis answered. "You can come here with me."

Reluctantly, Nish dismounted. "Personally," he muttered, "I'd rather take my chances with the bears."

They pushed their bikes up the long, overgrown

72

laneway, the grass in the middle so high it was a wonder anyone could drive through. Travis listened for the first bark of the dog, but there was no sound.

He looked around for a car, or a half-ton truck, but could find none. Perhaps he was out. More likely, however, he had no car and Muck was picking him up and dropping him off. That would be just like Muck.

There were orange irises growing on one side of the laneway, but they had never been tended to – or at least not for years. They weren't at all like the irises in Travis's grandmother's garden, and yet in their own way they were spectacular, almost as if their survival here gave them a doubled beauty. A few of the irises had recently been cut, the stems sliced off as neatly as if a razor blade had swept through them.

All around were rusted metal bars, old bedsprings, tires, car engines, a fishing boat with the bottom rotted clean through and, surprisingly, an old homemade lacrosse net made out of galvanized steel plumbing pipes and covered with burlap instead of netting. The burlap was rotting off. The net hadn't been used for years.

Travis edged his way up to the rickety porch that hung off the main building. It looked like it was held in place by old Scotch tape rather than nails. The boards were soft and gave. He wondered if he might fall through.

"*I'm outta here!*" hissed Nish.

"You're not going anywhere," Travis whispered quickly.

Nish was sweating as heavily as if he were in full goaltender's equipment and playing the third period of a lacrosse game. His face was beet-red and twisted in a grimace. Travis would have expected nothing less.

Travis arrived at the door. It was open a crack. There were flies – bluebottles, mosquitoes, horseflies, deerflies – all around the opening, but it was impossible to tell whether they were trying to get in or out. From what little Travis could make out in the dark, he wouldn't blame them for trying to escape. The floor was filthy and littered with junk. It was dark and it smelled of greasy cooking and kerosene and something else, something familiar.

Travis took one look back at his sweating pal and realized what the odour was: stale human sweat, worse than a lacrosse dressing room.

His heart pounding, Travis swallowed, took one deep breath, and knocked.

The boys waited. No movement. No barking. Nothing.

Travis knocked again, this time rapping his knuckles a little harder on the old door, which swung open slightly. He jumped back, afraid he'd be accused of just walking in.

But there was nothing.

"Thank God," breathed Nish. "He's not home."

Travis stepped back. "I guess not," he said. He didn't know if he was disappointed or not. He didn't like the idea of having to come out here again.

"But he specifically said this afternoon," Travis said.

"I guess he forgot," Nish said, seeming greatly relieved. "Let's go."

"Let's just check around back first," Travis suggested.

He caught Nish's look. It was as if he'd suggested they both do a little extra math homework or stay after school to help. A look of absolute, disbelieving disgust. But Travis knew Nish would be too afraid – both of Mr. Fontaine and the bears – to strike out on his own for home. He would have to wait for Travis, no matter what.

"Hurry it up, then," Nish hissed. "I haven't got all day. I'm a busy man."

Travis led the way around the side, shaking his head. What on earth could Nish mean, "I'm a busy man"? Was his cellphone ringing? Did he have to take a private jet to Hollywood? This movie stuff had gone to his head – and all they had was a little footage of three bears fighting over a garbage bag.

"It won't take long," Travis said in a whisper over his shoulder. He was still listening for the dog, once again wishing that instead of the lacrosse ball he had thought to stash a rock in his pocket, just in case. But still there was nothing. Not a sound anywhere but for the buzzing flies.

They turned around the side of the building, following a well-worn track. There were sheds out here, machine sheds and hay sheds and what must once have been animal sheds. He could still, faintly, smell the distinct odour of chicken and horse manure. But it seemed old. Very old. Decades old, for all Travis knew.

He checked each shed, but found no one. He dipped his head into what was obviously the tool shed and noticed a lamp burning – a coal-oil lamp, its wick flickering in the slight breeze that slipped in through the door. Travis knew that Mr. Fontaine must be around, or must have been around not long ago.

He turned to tell Nish that the shed was empty, that they could go home now. But Nish, moments ago as red as the bell on his mountain bike, was now as white as a sheet. His mouth seemed frozen open. He was pointing off into the bushes.

There, in the distance, someone was kneeling beneath a tall hemlock. Travis could tell from the man's back, the long grey-white hair, the thick eyeglasses, the old grey shirt, that it was Zeke Fontaine. He seemed to be picking at something on the ground. He was flicking off pebbles and small branches, carefully arranging something on the earth. Something orange.

Irises!

Travis quickly looked at Nish again. His friend was still white, but his mouth had become unfrozen, and he was carefully mouthing something to him.

A grave!

Zeke Fontaine was arranging flowers over a grave. The ground had been cleared under the hemlock and carefully swept. A rough rectangle of earth rose slightly above the surrounding ground, the space not quite as large as a plot at the local cemetery. But big enough for a boy.

Liam Fontaine's grave?

Travis shuddered. Was this the secret burial place of little Liam Fontaine? Was this what the father had done with the body after he had murdered his own son?

Travis and Nish exchanged a look of terror. It was time to get out of there. Travis turned quickly, and stepped onto a dry, dead twig.

SNAP!

"*We're dead meat!*" Nish hissed.

Travis felt what little blood there was left in his face drain to his feet. He nearly went down with it, instantly dizzy, in full panic.

"*Hey!*" a voice called out. "*Just stay right where you are!*"

14

THE YELL FROM UNDER THE HIGH HEMLOCK froze both boys in their path. Neither dared move. Travis could almost hear the rifle go off, feel the bullet finally quiet his heart, smell the earth as it was shovelled in on him as he and Nish joined Liam in the shallow grave, feel the weight of the irises crushing down on his shattered, bleeding chest.

"*Hey!*" the voice called again. "*That you, Travis?*"

Zeke Fontaine was up and walking towards them, moving surprisingly quickly for an old man. He wasn't going to shoot them, he would strangle them!

"*Travis?*" the old man called.

"Y-y-yes," Travis answered.

"I don't see too well no more," the old man said as he neared them. "But I could pick out your buddy at a hundred paces – goalie equipment or no goalie equipment."

"H-hi M-Mister F-F-Fontaine," stammered Nish.

"Glad you came," Mr. Fontaine said, clipping

both boys lightly on the shoulder. "I was just out fixing up the grave."

Travis and Nish exchanged the quickest of glances, but Zeke Fontaine's eyesight was not so poor that he didn't catch them. "Dog died two weeks ago," he explained. "He was seventeen years old. You know how old that is in our years, Nishikawa?"

"N–no sir."

"One hundred and nineteen, that's what. Seventeen years old and blind as a bat and even fewer teeth than me."

Zeke Fontaine peeled back his lips so the boys could see his teeth. The three or four that still stood were dark from cavities, his gums red and sore-looking. Travis had to look away.

"Wh–what about the sign?" Nish asked.

"The sign? Oh, yes, 'Beware of dog.' I put that up to inspire him. Sparky wouldn't have hurt a fly, which may explain why there are so many of the damn things around here."

Sparky, thought Travis. Sparky, not Liam. An old dog, not a boy. An old dog with fresh-cut irises on his carefully tended grave.

How could he have been so wrong?

They stayed more than an hour at Zeke Fontaine's. He went into the house and returned with chocolate bars and glasses – remarkably clean glasses – and as they ate their chocolate he took them over

79

to the well. He lowered the bucket and drew up water so cold and fresh and delicious that Travis thought if they could ever bottle it and sell it they would make millions.

"Glad you came along," Mr. Fontaine said to Nish. "I've been thinking about teaching you boys the 'Muck Munro.'"

"The 'Muck Munro'?" they said at once.

"He's never told you about it?"

Both boys shook their heads.

"He'd perfected it just before the championship, you know. Never got a chance to show it."

Travis nodded, afraid to say anything. What, after all, could he say? *Oh yes, never got to play in the championship because you murdered your son and it was all called off.*

"Muck and my boy . . . ," Mr. Fontaine began.

Travis and Nish both flinched. They hadn't expected the old man to mention Liam.

"Muck and my boy worked on this play until they could do it in their sleep. You want me to show it to you?"

"Yeah!" Nish said enthusiastically.

"You got your sticks here?" the old man asked.

"They're on our bikes," said Travis.

"Well, go get 'em. I'll get mine."

Travis and Nish hurried back to where they had laid down their bikes.

"He's not such a bad old guy," Nish offered.

"No," said Travis, a bit ashamed of the surprise in his voice.

Mr. Fontaine was walking back from the house with his old Logan stick in his hand. Travis was getting used to the sight of the wooden stick now, and in fact had decided it was beautiful compared to his own with its plastic head.

"You remember that bounce play I taught you?" Zeke Fontaine said to Travis.

"Sure," Travis said. "Use it all the time."

"Well, Muck Munro had that one mastered, too. My God, but he was a fine young player – one of the two best I ever saw."

Travis bit his tongue, hoping that Nish wouldn't dare ask who the other great prospect was. They both knew the answer: Liam Fontaine.

"Muck would use the bounce play a few times a game. Then I taught him this little trick we used to call the 'Muck Munro.'"

Mr. Fontaine was already wrestling the old net out of the mess of rusting metal scrap in the yard. He placed it in front of the tool shed, where the ground was trampled smooth and hard, nearly as hard as a concrete floor.

"You're our goaltender," Mr. Fontaine said to Nish. "So get in here."

"Now, Travis," he continued, "you're last man back and I'm coming in. Give me that ball."

Travis threw the ball, and the old man plucked it out of the air like a cat playing with a floating milkweed seed. It made absolutely no sound, but when the stick ceased to spin, there was the ball, nestled in the pocket as neatly as if it had been placed there by hand. It was something Travis never tired of seeing.

The old man felt the heft of the ball, threw a few fakes, and ran out in a short loop before coming in on Travis. He feinted once, then forced Travis's feet apart with the shoulder fake and bounced the ball clean between Travis's legs, floating effortlessly around him to catch it coming up, fake a backhand, and then slip a slow underhand behind the sprawling Nish.

"*Nice goal!*" Nish shouted.

"But I wouldn't be able to do it all the time," the old man said, twirling the ball out of the net and back into his old Logan. He came up and stood side by side with Travis, acting as if both were defenders on the same play. "You'd learn to expect it. You'd fall for it once or twice, maybe three times, and next time you'd keep your feet together and block the bounce, wouldn't you?"

"I guess I would," said Travis.

"Sure you would," said Mr. Fontaine. "So you need to come up with a new trick. Keep your feet together this time and I'll show you the 'Muck Munro,' okay?"

Again the old man set out in his easy loop. He turned, smiled once, and then came in on Travis.

Travis saw the shoulder fake, but refused to

move his feet, watching for the bounce pass so he could block it.

But there was nothing, only a gentle whisper high over Travis's head. As he looked up he caught sight of the old man, still smiling, nothing whatsoever in his hands, peeling by him on the outside.

Travis was so surprised, he lost his balance. He slipped on the hard earth and fell backwards, jarring his tailbone as he hit the ground. Behind him he could see, upside down, the old man reach up and catch his floating stick. He faked once, twice, then worked a gentle sidearm past Nish on the short side.

Nish was laughing so hard he couldn't even try for it. He fell in a heap on the earth, howling and holding his sides.

Travis, too, began to laugh.

"Wh–what happened?" he asked.

"Nothing," the old man said. "Just the 'Muck Munro,' that's all."

The old man had the ball back in his stick. He was smiling. "This time just watch," he said.

Both boys took up their positions. The old man did his lazy loop again, and as he turned, Travis noticed how he took one hand off his stick and wedged the ball down hard into the pocket.

He came in, tried the shoulder fake, and then threw the stick high over Travis's head so that it stayed upright, seeming to float through the air as he moved around Travis, reached up and grabbed the handle again.

The old man shook the stick hard, once, and the jammed ball popped free, ready for the fake and an easy goal.

Never had they imagined anything so magical, never had they seen anything quite so lovely as the upright stick, spinning through the air like a long, skinny top that didn't even need a surface over which to dance.

Zeke Fontaine threw Travis the ball. "Your turn," he commanded.

The old man took up Travis's place on defence, Nish resumed his spot in the net, and Travis set out on his own lazy loop before turning.

Travis tried, discreetly, to jam the ball into the bottom of his pocket. But it wouldn't stick. He came in on the old man, faked, and then, when Mr. Fontaine went to block the bounce play, he tossed the stick high. The ball spun out the moment he let go of the stick.

Nish caught the lost ball.

The old man turned, his face puzzled.

"Let me see that," the old man said, as Travis picked up his stick.

Travis was confused. "See what?"

"Your stick," Mr. Fontaine said. "Let me have a look at it."

Travis handed it over and the old man examined it carefully. He jammed the ball down into the pocket, then tossed the stick high with a spin. But the ball flew free. Travis felt a little better; at least it hadn't been just him.

The old man took his own stick in one hand and Travis's in the other and glanced back and forth between the two. Finally he dropped Travis's Brine.

"Damn modern sticks," the old man said. "Sorry, boys, didn't mean to swear, but look at this."

The two boys drew closer. Mr. Fontaine jammed the ball into his own stick. It pushed aside the catgut at the bottom and wedged tight to the wood. He spun the stick and the ball stayed locked in the pocket. Then he picked up Travis's stick and tried the same thing. Since the head was entirely hard plastic there was no flexibility. He couldn't wedge the ball into place.

"You got to have the catgut," the old man said, as if confirming something he already knew. "You can't do it with these plastic jobbies. You got to have the real thing – a Logan."

He turned back to Travis. "Would you play with a Logan if you had one?"

Travis swallowed hard. "Yes, sir," he said, "I would."

For a moment Travis thought he was about to be given Mr. Fontaine's own stick, but Mr. Fontaine clearly had something else in mind. "There's a Logan in the house that's practically brand new," the old man said. "Used one summer only." He paused, to correct himself. "Used *part* of one summer."

Travis felt a tremor in his back. Used part of one summer? A Logan, practically new?

"Come in here a minute," Mr. Fontaine said. He turned and headed towards the house, obviously expecting the boys to follow. Travis looked at Nish. Nish looked at Travis. Then both turned and followed him into the house, as they had been asked.

The flies buzzed around them. Travis swatted a mosquito. The old man was rooting about in what seemed to be a shed tacked on to the back of the main house. An open doorway to one side led to what looked like it might be the living room. There were papers all over the place.

Mr. Fontaine grunted with satisfaction and stepped back, pulling a lacrosse stick out from a pile of shovels and rakes that were leaning against the wall. He turned, punching the pocket, wiping a hand up and down the handle to clear away the dust.

Dust or not, Travis could tell it was a Logan. Barely used. Still as good as the day it was bought, thirty or forty years before.

"You think you can take good care of this?" the old man asked as he handed it over to Travis.

"Yes, sir," Travis said. "It's beautiful."

"It belonged to my boy," Zeke Fontaine said.

"He was Muck's best friend. And as good a lacrosse player as I've ever seen in my life."

The old man sounded so sad as he said this. Travis had no idea what to say to him.

"He sounds like a neat kid," Nish said, filling in the gap.

The old man nodded. He looked up, his old eyes glistening in the dim light. "There's a picture of him there on that table," he said, pointing a slightly shaking finger.

It was an old school picture, now badly faded, but it showed a handsome young man with light blond hair and a wide, confident smile.

"Looks about our age," Nish said.

The old man nodded.

Travis could say nothing. He was dumbstruck. He stood, his mouth wide open, staring at the photograph of Liam Fontaine.

He felt he had seen the boy before . . . somewhere.

At the graveyard?

15

FOR THE ENTIRE RIDE BACK TO TOWN TRAVIS wondered how to tell Nish that he thought he had seen Liam Fontaine before. He had no idea how he could say *anything* without making a complete fool of himself. What could he say? That he had seen the boy at the cemetery the night they had gone to *The Blood Children: Part VIII*. Nish wouldn't believe him. And who would blame him? Travis couldn't believe it himself.

It made no sense.

Nish, however, was thinking only about his movie. He babbled all the way about the "great setting" Old Man Fontaine's place would make for a horror flick. Nish loved the dark, spooky house. Loved the dog's grave. Loved Zeke Fontaine's face — so much in fact that he was even toying with asking the old man if he'd like a part in his film.

Get real! Travis wanted to say. But he said nothing. He let Nish dream on. And he tried to force his own thoughts back to something more down-to-earth.

The Screech Owls were due to play the following evening in Brantford, home of the second-best team in the league, the Warriors. It was going to be a tough test for the Owls. If they could compete against the Warriors, they were a real lacrosse team.

Travis wondered if he had enough courage to try the stick Mr. Fontaine had given him. The Warriors were everything Muck had warned

them they would be. Big and tough and extremely skilled, if a bit slow on their feet. Mr. Dillinger seemed particularly worried and fidgeted terribly, almost as if he wished he had something useful to do – like sharpen skates. But Mr. Dillinger only had water bottles to fill and laces to worry about, and the lack of work just seemed to make him more nervous.

Travis, too, was nervous. He took the new – or was it old? – Logan out for warm-up and one of the referees came running over to check it out. Not because it might be illegal, as Travis first feared, but because he had recognized the make and wanted a closer look.

"You're a lucky young man," he said to Travis as he handed it back.

Travis wasn't so sure.

The game began. Sarah won the draw easily, but was instantly flattened by a hard check from behind. The ball squirted to Travis's side and he tried to scoop it up but lost it when it ticked off the catgut. A Warrior scooped it free, tossed it cross-floor, and sent in his winger on a break. He rolled right off Fahd's check and scored easily on a bounce shot that Nish misjudged.

One shot, one goal.

The Warriors built the score to 5–0 by the time of the first intermission. Travis and the other Owls sagged against the boards, spraying water directly onto their faces and munching on orange sections that Mr. Dillinger had cut up when he ran out of other things to do.

Travis was disheartened. The Owls looked weak and disorganized and unskilled.

"Your speed," Muck said. "Use your speed."

Sarah got them rolling with a great rush up-floor in which she turned her back on the defence as they came together, crashed into them, and dropped off to Dmitri, who stepped around the falling defenders and beat the Brantford goalie on a sidearm.

Andy scored on a long shot that took an odd bounce.

Simon scored on a shot that tipped in off a Warrior's stick.

The Warriors scored two more, and the Owls answered with two, one by Sam and the other by Travis on a low underhand that skimmed the floor and slipped right in between the Brantford goalie's feet.

They were into the third frame, the Owls still down by two goals, when Wilson scored on a wonderful solo effort that took him up-floor and around the opposition net, sending in a high overhand lob that just cleared the goaltender's shoulder before the clock ran out.

There was only a minute left in the game.

Sarah had the ball in her own corner. Two Warriors were on her. She huddled down and popped the ball free to Nish, who'd left his crease to help out.

Travis cut towards centre. "NISH!" he screamed.

Nish saw him and hit him perfectly. Travis took the ball, turned, and headed in.

One defender back.

Travis reached up and wedged the ball down hard into the pocket. He had tried the bounce play twice already. Once it had worked. Once it hadn't. They might be expecting it again.

He dropped his shoulder.

The defender didn't go for it, keeping his legs together to block any bounce.

Travis tossed his stick, high and spinning through the air, and stepped around the surprised defenceman. The stick seemed to move in slow motion. It hung suspended in the air. Travis could hear gasps from the crowd. He could hear his own feet slapping on the floor.

Moving in under the stick, he reached up with one hand and caught it. He jammed the stick down so the bottom of the handle rapped off the arena floor, jiggling the ball free.

A fake, a fake backhander, and he slipped an underhand shot in the short side.

The arena erupted.

The players on the floor mobbed Travis. The players on the bench bolted as the clock ran out and the buzzer sounded.

Travis had scored a thousand goals in hockey, including practices, exhibition games, and road games, but it was never like this.

Even Nish was on top of him, weighing about fifty extra pounds in his sweat-filled, stinking equipment. He had never smelled so sweet!

Now there were other hands pulling him free. Strong, big hands. It was Muck. He was smiling and shaking his head. "I guess I know where you got that."

Travis smiled back. He looked for Mr. Fontaine, but the old man was already at the gate leading off the floor and away.

There was no use chasing him. The players were all holding each other and half dancing in the corner of the rink. They had only tied the game, but they had tied the *Warriors*.

They were a team.

A competitive team.

With only the championship now to go.

16

"IT'S NO GOOD."

Travis didn't like what he was hearing, but wasn't surprised. Data and Fahd and Sarah and Sam were delivering the verdict on the video he and Nish had brought back from the dump.

"You can see too much of the dump," said Fahd.

"No one's going to be scared out of their wits by a bear ripping apart a garbage bag," said Data.

"We're going to have to try again," said Sarah.

Travis let out a long breath. "Okay," he said. "What can we do?"

Sam had some ideas. They would set up in the deep woods just behind the dump and try to film one of the bears in the wild. They could then combine this with the better shots of the bears taking swipes and runs at each other in the dump, but only the ones that didn't show the garbage.

Fahd jumped in: "And we can do a third series of shots showing dummies being ripped apart or blowing up or whatever. If we edit them in, people will think the bears are ripping people up. We just need to find a few dummies."

"No problem there," Sam said, looking right at him.

Fahd had heard the joke before, but still didn't get it.

"Fine!" Nish interrupted. "There's only one problem. How do we find a bear in the woods?"

"He comes to us," Sam said. "You have to *attract* them — that's what hunters do."

"We're not going to *shoot* them!" said Data.

"Yes we are," said Sam, "with a camera."

"Hunters bait them," said Simon. "They put out rotting meat."

"*Gross!*" said several of the Owls together.

"The bears are attracted by the smell," Simon continued. "It has to be a strong smell, that's why they use meat that's gone bad."

"Where are we going to find a smell *that* powerful?" wailed Fahd.

"Think about it," said Sam.

There was a pause. No one understood.

Sam slowly raised her hand and very deliberately pointed, as if she were taking aim, at the source of a smell powerful enough to attract the attention of wild bears.

Nish!

Travis thought to himself, It's a good thing that we're capturing this on film, otherwise no one would ever believe it!

They were deep in the bush behind the garbage dump. They knew they were in the right area when Jesse found a large beech tree with sharp, regularly spaced scrapings across the bark. "A bear has scratched here to sharpen his claws," he announced.

Travis looked up, way up. For a bear to reach that high, it would have to be twice the height of Travis. At least. He shuddered.

"*What's this?*" Nish called from farther up the trail.

The others hurried along. Nish was standing over a huge black mound of what looked, on first glance, like mud.

"Bear dropping," said Jesse.

Nish giggled. "How come *we* don't call it 'dropping'?"

"Because most of us have the decency to use a toilet," said Sam.

"At least this proves a bear has been here recently," said Simon.

"Time to get ready, Stinker Boy," said Sarah.

All eyes were now on Nish. He was, already sweating. His face was twisted like an old sock.

"We're *not* going to do this," he wailed.

"We are so," said Sam. "Now get your stuff on!"

17

AND THAT WAS HOW WAYNE NISHIKAWA CAME to be walking down a bush trail in full lacrosse goalie equipment. He looked a bit like a bear himself, the heavy equipment nearly doubling his bulk and making him waddle as he walked.

Sam's idea had been ingenious, Travis thought. They needed a terrific, horrific smell that no bear on earth could help but notice. What better than Nish's lacrosse equipment?

Nish had been outraged. He was furious when Sam suggested it and fought the idea tooth and nail. But the Owls had thought about it and decided. In the end, he had no choice. The horror movie, after all, was his idea. If it was going to work, they all had to pitch in – and this time it was his turn.

"*I'm the director!*" he'd whined. "*Not bear bait!*"

Jesse and Simon, who knew more about the bush than the others, had taken over the rest of the planning. Jesse knew, from experience, that nothing gets rid of a black bear better than a sudden sound, so they were carrying whistles, and Jesse even had an old pot and a wooden spoon to smack together if they needed to drive one off.

"*What if one of them starts to eat me?*" Nish had whined.

"What's '*I'm gonna hurl!*' in bear language?" laughed Sarah.

"Don't worry about it," said Jesse. "Bears are a lot more scared of people than people should be of them."

Nish had dressed, reluctantly, at the side of the road and then walked in with the rest to take up their positions. He would waddle along the trails in his stinking equipment; Jesse and Simon would be right behind him in case some sudden noise was needed; and the Owls would set up with their cameras in two strategic places, hoping to get some good footage of a black bear rambling through the woods. With luck, they'd even have one of them rise on its haunches to sniff the air for some stinking Nishikawa.

Travis and Sarah and Sam were to take the far end of the path. Fahd and Andy were among the Owls at the near end.

Travis found a perfect stand of cedar to wriggle into. The branches were soft and smelled wonderful, and the skirt of the cedar was so low and dense that, once he was inside, he could not be seen from the trail.

Sarah and Sam hunkered down on the other side of the trail. Sam had the video camera. If either Travis or Sarah saw signs of a bear coming, their job was to alert Sam to be ready.

It was a hot, lazy day. There were still mosquitoes in the woods, and Travis wished he'd remembered to bring along a bottle of bug repellent. He felt he was being eaten alive.

The wind was still. The only sounds were the occasional songbird flitting through the trees, the grating call of a crow high in the maples, and as the air grew hotter, the deep, long buzz of cicadas that seemed to come from nowhere and everywhere at the same time.

Travis thought he heard a whistle!

It could mean one of only two things: a bear had been spotted, or a bear had to be frightened off.

He listened hard, wondering if he put his ear to the ground whether he could hear the sound better, the way a railway track is supposed to let you know a train is coming long before it can be seen.

He could hear breathing now! Heavy breathing, puffing!

Travis pushed out a little from under the apron of cedar branches. He looked down the trail, the sunlight dancing as it played through the high branches and spotted the path with occasional bright patches.

The sound was closer now! And he could hear branches being pushed aside and then swishing back into place.

He could hear grunting! The telltale sound of Nish working hard.

Travis looked across at Sarah and Sam. Sam was readying the camera. Sarah was leaning down, staring towards the sound of the oncoming Nish.

The branch of a spruce was thrust aside, and Nish pushed through, breathing very heavily now. He wasn't running, but he seemed anxious, frightened.

Travis suddenly felt sorry for his friend.

Nish kept going, past Sam, past Sarah, past Travis, completely unaware that they were hidden there in the bush.

The spruce bough swung again, this time more slowly.

Travis felt his breath catch.

The head of a bear pushed through, swinging its nose from side to side, sniffing for Nish!

Travis could see Sam already filming. She was well out of sight and downwind from the bear. It hadn't noticed her.

The bear pushed the rest of the way through. It was huge!

It paused, sniffed the air again, then rose on its haunches.

Travis caught the briefest flash of white.

Silvertip!

18

WHERE WERE JESSE AND SIMON?

Travis frantically searched the dark shadows beyond the bear. There was neither sight nor sound of them.

Perhaps the whistle had been a warning to scare off the big bear, but hadn't worked! Perhaps the two boys had become separated from Nish or taken a wrong turn.

Maybe Nish *was* running! Maybe that was as fast as he could go with all that equipment on!

Travis instantly regretted this whole wild scheme. They should never have agreed to send Nish out in his equipment. It might have seemed funny at the time – but no longer.

The bear settled on all fours again, sniffed and grunted loudly.

"HHHELLLLLP!"

The call came from ahead on the path. Travis swung around and saw that Nish had turned and seen the bear up on his hind legs. Nish was still wearing his goaltender's mask, but the cage over his face couldn't hide the pure, absolute terror in his eyes.

"HHHELLLLLP MMMMEEEE!"

Travis acted at once. His friend had called and he had to respond. He leaped free of his cover and jumped up and down, waving his arms.

"SHOOOO!" he shouted. "GET AWAY, BEAR!"

The bear stopped, rose again on his haunches.

Travis knew at once he'd made a mistake. He'd have had better luck against mosquitoes with that silly shout than against the biggest bear in the woods.

"SCRAMMMM!" he shouted with more force. He picked up a branch and threw it, spinning and crashing through the air. He wished he'd had a rock in his pocket. He looked around but could see none on the soft, needle-covered earth.

Silvertip stared at Travis, then raised his nose, sniffing. Sniffing for me? Travis wondered. Or sniffing for Nish?

Silvertip settled, then turned, his huge shoulders snapping dead twigs as he changed direction and headed off the path.

Straight for Travis.

"TRAVISSS!" Sarah shouted. "GET OUT OF HERE, QUICK!"

Travis was running before he could even think. He was pushing through spruce and cedar, the branches whipping into his face, and he was stumbling and sliding and slipping up and down hills.

He knew it was wrong. He knew that one thing you were never supposed to do around a black bear was turn tail and run. Back away slowly, the park rangers always said. Make noise, show no fear, and back away slowly. Don't panic, don't show them you're petrified – and never run away screaming.

But that's just what Travis Lindsay did.

Silvertip sniffed the air again and then picked up his pace, heading straight in the direction Travis had just taken.

"GO, TRAVISSSS!" Sam called.

Travis thought he was in good shape from lacrosse, but he had never tired so quickly in his life. He was covered in sweat. It was stinging the scrapes from the branches and raspberry bushes. He had dirt in his eyes. But he was still moving.

He crashed through the bush, down a dried-up creek, and up a small hill. He leaped over rocks, used roots to pull himself higher, swung onto a bluff and kept on running.

Travis's lungs were killing him. He stopped, just for a moment, to catch his breath and look back.

Silvertip was still coming!

Travis hurdled logs and crashed through bogs and stumbled over stones, but he kept going.

He no longer needed to look back to see if the bear was following.

He could hear it behind him.

The big bear grunted like a pig. He crashed through the bush as if it were made of paper, not hardwood and rock. He snapped branches and ripped aside logs and sent rocks churning down slopes.

Travis leaped up a small hill and over a fallen tree and came – suddenly – to a dead end.

He could go no farther.

Ahead was open air, and thirty feet straight down was a tangle of rock and stumps and dead branches.

Silvertip was already on the hill, grunting heavily, crashing through everything in his path.

Travis had no choice. He had to jump. There was a soft ledge about halfway down. If he could land on that he might roll safely to a stop. He might even be able to stay there, out of reach of the bear.

He had no time to think. No time to cry or pray. He just leaped.

He felt the air cool on his face, welcome on his scrapes. He felt himself floating through the air, moving so slowly he almost believed he was taking flight.

Then he crashed into the ledge.

It no longer looked, or felt, so soft.

He hit hard and rolled, paused for a moment on the edge, then dropped again, heading for the bottom.

19

TRAVIS HAD NO IDEA HOW LONG HE HAD LAIN there. He knew he was hurt. His left hand was throbbing. He felt his legs, moved them both, flexed his feet. They were fine.

He looked up to the top of the bluff.

Silvertip was standing there, staring down!

Travis had no more strength left to run. Something sticky was on his face and dripping down onto his lips. He tested it with his tongue. *Blood!*

Instinctively, with his right hand, he fumbled for a stone to protect himself. He stared up at the bear, and the bear stared back, sniffing the air.

Travis felt a large, round rock and tucked it in tight to his chest. If the bear comes down, he thought, I might be able to scare him off with one good throw. But I'll only have one chance.

Silvertip backed off.

He's looking for a way down! Travis thought.

He was crying. He was crying for his parents and his grandparents and for Muck and Mr. Dillinger. Crying for Nish and Sarah and all his teammates. Crying because they'd been so foolish.

He could hear the bear grunting, hear the slide of gravel and stone as the huge beast began coming down the side.

He drew the rock back, ready to throw.

CLANG! CLANG! CLANG! CLANG! CLANG!

What was that sound?

Travis shook his head, trying to get a fix on it.

CLANG! CLANG! CLANG! CLANG! CLANG!

Jesse's pot! The wooden spoon on the old pot!

Now there was a whistle. Then another. Loud and shrill.

There was movement in the cedars. First Jesse pushed through, still banging, then Simon with his whistle blasting, then Sarah and Sam, with the camera still filming, and finally Nish, his helmet off and his face redder and wetter than Travis had ever seen it.

"*He's over to your right!*" Travis called.

They looked to where Travis thought he had heard the bear coming down.

"*He's long gone!*" Jesse shouted down to him.

"*Stay there, Travis,*" shouted Sarah. "*We're coming to get you!*"

Travis felt his first full breath enter his lungs. He could feel his hand hurting now, his skin was stinging, but he felt absolutely wonderful.

Silvertip was gone!

He set his rock down, already smiling at his own foolishness. *As if this would have stopped Silvertip!* he said to himself, looking at it.

It was an oddly shaped thing, perfectly round on one side, jagged on the other, and not all that heavy for its size. He almost threw it away before catching himself.

It wasn't a rock at all!

Travis stared at it, not believing what he held in his hand.

A human skull!

20

"THE REMAINS HAVE BEEN IDENTIFIED AS THOSE of Liam Fontaine, a twelve-year-old Tamarack boy who disappeared under mysterious circumstances more than thirty years ago."

Travis was not surprised to hear the newscast confirm what everyone in town already known. The provincial police had called in the forensic investigation unit from Toronto, and more bones had been found in the rubble and rotting branches where Travis had landed when he fell down the bluff.

It was not a shallow grave. It was typical of a black bear cache, a kill hidden under branches and leaves and partially covered with earth. Teeth marks on the skull and several bones clearly indicated that the youngster had been killed by a rogue bear.

Zeke Fontaine had not, as so many had believed, killed his son.

Travis was taken to the hospital, cleaned up, checked over, X-rayed, and released. His left hand still hurt, but the doctors said he could play lacrosse if he wanted, so long as he was careful not to use his hand too much.

There was no more talk about a movie. No one wanted to make the ninth episode of *The Blood Children* or even the first episode of *The Killer Bears of Tamarack*. Now that they knew the truth, it seemed wrong to think about Liam Fontaine's fate as a plot for a made-up story, and none of the Owls ever again mentioned it – not even Nish, the director.

All the Owls wanted to do now was concentrate on lacrosse, and they were happy to have a practice to go to the next day. Even so, they had trouble concentrating on breakouts and defence patterns and the like. Travis, in particular, found it hard to keep his thoughts on the game.

Two newspapers from Toronto had sent reporters to talk to him and the other Owls involved in the find. No one, mercifully, had mentioned Nish's ridiculous movie or how he came to be wandering through the deep woods dressed in his lacrosse goaltending equipment. That would have been just too hard to explain.

And now there was a television camera at the practice. Travis was wondering what effect the camera might have on Nish when he noticed a couple of familiar figures standing behind the seats, watching.

One was his grandfather, who rarely came to

games and had never, ever been to a practice.

The other was old Mr. Donahue from the Autumn Leaves Retirement Home.

Muck ended the practice with a team run around the boards, first clockwise, then counter-clockwise, then in a long figure–eight pattern with the players crossing at centre floor lobbing a ball back and forth to the nearest passing teammate.

Travis was exhausted. After Muck blew the whistle to signal practice was finished, Travis loped over to where Mr. Fontaine was hauling the water bottles out of the players' box. He picked one up and sprayed the water directly into his face. Travis had come over deliberately. He still hadn't said anything to Mr. Fontaine.

"How's the Logan?" Mr. Fontaine asked, smiling.

"Fine," Travis said. "I love it." He didn't know what else to say.

Mr. Fontaine looked younger. He no longer seemed so white, so stooped. No longer seemed as if he were trying to disappear as he walked.

Mr. Dillinger was holding the door open for them to leave the floor and head for the dressing rooms. Mr. Fontaine went first, Travis right behind him.

His grandfather and Mr. Donahue were waiting.

Mr. Fontaine kept his head down, though Travis knew he must have recognized the two former policemen.

"Do you have a moment, Zeke?" Travis's grandfather said.

The old lacrosse coach stopped, fidgeting with the water bottles he was carrying. He seemed to have trouble looking at the two men.

"Ed and I just want to say how sorry we are," old Mr. Lindsay was saying. He had his hand out, waiting.

Slowly, old Mr. Fontaine reached for the hand of the former policeman who had always believed something else had happened to little Liam Fontaine.

Muck wanted to speak to them.

He had never done this before. Muck speaking to them before a game was rare. Muck speaking to them after a game was almost unheard-of. Muck speaking to them after a practice was unimaginable.

Nish was lying flat on his back on the floor. He had his mask off and was holding a water bottle directly over his head, spraying hard. Sam and Sarah were also on their backs on the floor, their legs resting on the bench. Mr. Fontaine had said it was a great way to get the blood flowing right again.

"Saturday morning we start the tournament,"

Muck said. "We're the hosts and, naturally, we don't want to let the town down. That means you're expected to behave well in addition to playing well. Got that, Mr. Nishikawa?"

"Got it, Coach!" Nish called from the floor, still spraying water in his face.

Muck frowned. He hated being called "Coach," which only made Nish do it all the more.

"When we began the season we didn't know much about this game," Muck said. "I think we owe Mr. Fontaine here a vote of thanks for helping us out."

The dressing room erupted with cheers.

"Our aim is to provide some real competition," Muck said, "and when we played against Brantford, we proved we can do it. Mr. Fontaine has another thought, though, and I'd like you to hear it from him, if you don't mind."

Mr. Fontaine swallowed hard and stepped to the centre of the floor.

Even Nish was paying attention now, his empty water bottle held to his chest like a newborn baby.

Mr. Fontaine cleared his throat. He rapped his old Logan stick once on the floor.

"We can win it," he said.

Nothing more. And certainly nothing less.

We can win it.

21

THE PROVINCIAL PEEWEE CHAMPIONSHIP BEGAN in Tamarack on a Saturday morning so hot there was some concern Nish might melt entirely away. He sweated so much in game one against the Niagara Falls Thunder that several times the officials had to blow down play and get the arena staff to come out with squeegees and clear off the water around the Screech Owls' crease.

Nish had good cause to sweat. The Thunder was a good team, fast rushing and smart with the ball. But for Nish's extraordinary play the Owls would have fallen out of contention right from the opening whistle. Sarah and Travis and Dmitri also played their best game yet. Sarah ended the game with eight assists and a goal, Dmitri with seven goals and three assists, and Travis with four goals and four assists. The Owls won 14–9.

In game two they were up against a team from upstate New York, the Watertown Seaway. They won easily, 22–5, with Jesse Highboy leading the charge with four goals and four assists. Sarah had another four goals and three assists, and Travis and Dmitri both had two of each.

"You're leading the tournament in scoring," Jenny shouted back to Sarah as she scanned the results in the lobby. Sarah said nothing. She blushed and headed outside with Dmitri to toss the ball around between matches. Travis joined them, blinking as his eyes adjusted to the incredible brightness of the sun.

Mr. Fontaine was already out there. "C'mere for a moment, son," he said when he noticed Travis. "Let me see that stick again."

Travis handed over the precious Logan. Mr. Fontaine ran his bony hands up and down the shaft and over the pocket and along the catgut. He punched the pocket and felt the heft of the ball in it and punched the pocket again.

"You're shooting slightly high, you know," the old man said, adjusting his glasses on his nose.

Travis knew instantly that Mr. Fontaine was right. One of his goals had looked spectacular, the ball tipping in off the crossbar, but in fact he had intended to skip the ball in off the floor.

Mr. Fontaine's hands were fast at work. He was undoing the braiding and pulling and yanking the lines left and right. He put the heel of his foot in the pocket and pushed down hard, using the ground for leverage. He tried the ball again, adjusted the pocket again, then declared himself satisfied and rebraided the stick.

He handed it back to Travis. "Try an overhand fake."

The ball seemed to sag in the pocket. It felt odd, and for a moment Travis wished Mr. Fontaine had left the stick alone.

He tried the fake and was amazed at how it held in the pocket. He giggled. The old man giggled along with him.

"Try a full forehand fake," the old man said, "and let it become an underhand shot."

Travis didn't follow.

"Here," the old man said. "Watch me."

Mr. Fontaine took the ball and faked a couple of times to get the feel of it. Then he fired what looked like a hard overhand against the arena wall, but the ball held perfectly in the pocket. Mr. Fontaine let the stick swing almost in a full arc, past his left knee and towards his back, but at the last second it changed direction and he ripped a hard underhand that slapped off the wall and jumped back into his stick so fast it seemed he couldn't possibly have had time to catch it.

"*Wow!*" said Travis.

"Try it," Mr. Fontaine said with a grin.

Travis did, and lost the ball on the fake. He made a second attempt, and lost the ball when he tried to stop the arc and turn the stick. He lost it a third time on the shot.

But the fourth time he got it.

"It's yours now," the old man said. "You own that play."

22

JENNY STAPLES WAS AGAIN AT THE ROUND-ROBIN chart pasted up in the lobby. The Owls had won three games and tied one, and a tournament official was just now pencilling in the two teams that would meet in the championship game.

He wrote "SCREECH OWLS" above one line.

Then he began writing on the opposite side: "T-O-R . . ."

"Oh no!" wailed Jenny. "Not the Toronto Mini-Rock!"

But it was indeed. The Owls against the Mini-Rock, the team they had lost to 19–8 earlier in the summer. The biggest, meanest, toughest, nastiest, and *best* peewee team in the province.

The game was set for Saturday night at eight o'clock. "Prime time!" Nish called it. The local cable station was going to carry it live, and Nish was acting as if ESPN, TSN, Sportsnet, and Eurosport were all going to broadcast it.

"*Sports Illustrated* called," Nish told them as they dressed. "I got next week's cover."

It was as if the Owls had never before played a *real* lacrosse game. Travis had never felt the game move so quickly, never felt *himself* move so quickly. There was no time to think, no time to plan, only time to react – and right from the start the Mini-Rock were reacting quicker than the Screech Owls.

The big Toronto centre was again dominating Sarah. He used his strength and size to bowl her over on draws. He crushed her in the corners. He hassled her when she wasn't even in the play, and twice tripped her when she tried to break free. Not once did the referee call a penalty, which angered the Screech Owls' bench so much some of the players shouted at the referee.

"Enough of that!" Muck said, once.

Once was enough. Every player on the bench knew that Muck disapproved of catcalls. He always said, "Players win and lose games, officials don't."

The Mini-Rock went ahead 4–1 early in the match, the Owls' sole mark coming from little, skinny Fahd, who whipped a sidearm shot blind from the point and let it fly like a laser for an open corner of the net.

Muck kept pushing the Owls to use their speed, and it began to make a difference. Dmitri was sent in alone by Sarah, and double-faked the goalie flat onto his back before scoring the Screech Owls' second. Sam scored on a hard overhand that ticked off a Mini-Rock player's shoulder pads.

By the start of the third, the game was tied 9–9. The squeegee patrol was working overtime to keep Nish's crease clear of water, but it seemed the more he sweated the better he played. Several of Nish's stops had been unbelievable. He was clearing shots away with his stick to prevent rebounds and had developed a trick of falling backwards when he stopped a ball, flipping his stick high as he went down and sending the ball up into the rafters. A couple of times it even went over the netting at the back of the goal and sailed into the stands.

"He's showing off," Sarah said to Travis as they sat a shift.

"He's going to score on himself if he isn't careful," said Travis.

"He's brilliant," said Dmitri.

Both Sarah and Travis looked oddly at Dmitri.

"He's *Nish!*" both corrected at once.

Yet Travis had to admit that Nish *was* brilliant. He was playing the game of his life.

The Mini-Rock went ahead 13–11 on a string of goals and assists by the big centre.

"Speed," Muck kept saying. "Use your speed!"

Dmitri broke free and ran almost the entire length of the floor to score.

The officials called a time-out so the arena staff could mop up around Nish's crease. It was beginning to look like they needed a pump, as well as the squeegees.

Travis felt hands on his shoulders. He looked down. Long, bony fingers, white and wrinkled.

"Time for a little creativity, son," Mr. Fontaine said in Travis's ear.

Travis had tried his bounce pass, but he'd been knocked flying before he could step around the defence. His left hand was still a bit sore from the fall, so he'd been afraid to try the "Muck Munro"; if he botched it, the Mini-Rock would end up with the ball and he'd be lost, without his stick, at the other end.

But he still had the overhand fake.

Travis checked the clock.

Ninety seconds.

"*Sarah!*" Muck called out.

Sarah's line spilled over the boards. Travis punched his stick pocket a couple of times and lined up while Sarah took the draw.

"Get a *real* stick!" the winger opposite him called out.

Travis said nothing. It was to his advantage if the other side dismissed his Logan. The more he and his stick were underestimated, the better chance they'd have.

Sarah won the draw cleanly. She fired the ball back to Sam, who ran behind Nish's net and stood, using the goal as a guard.

The clock behind her was running down.

Sarah broke cross-floor and Sam hit her perfectly with a pass. Sarah passed – *backhand* – to Dmitri, who broke up the far boards and then cut for centre floor, slowing down the play.

Travis was coming up his wing. Dmitri backed into his check, protecting the ball, and looked for Travis. He flicked the ball quickly, straight into Travis's pocket.

The second defender rushed at Travis. He faked overhand as hard as he could.

It looked like a panic shot. The defender moved to block it. But Travis held the shot, turning his stick as it swung so it seemed impossible that the ball had stayed.

The Mini-Rock goaltender, convinced he'd missed it, looked quickly behind him to see if the shot had been so fast it was already in the net.

Travis held the arc and turned his stick just as it swung past his knee.

The ball was still in the pocket.

Quick as his wrists would reverse, Travis fired the ball underhand, the shot rising as it passed the surprised defenceman and came in on the even more surprised goaltender.

Ping!

In off the crossbar!

Mini-Rock 13, Owls 13.

Travis had tied the championship game with old man Fontaine's overhand fake!

23

THERE WAS NO TIME FOR CELEBRATION. THIRTY-
three seconds remained on the clock with a draw
at centre floor.

Again, Sarah took the draw and flipped it back
to Sam, who began another retreat behind Nish's
net. The Mini-Rock, however, had other ideas.
They put a two-player press on Sam, the two
closest forwards rushing her in the hopes of
causing a turnover or a panic throw.

Both forwards hit Sam at once. She buckled
under their cross-checks, but just as she went
down she managed to direct the ball towards
Nish's crease.

Nish raced forward, scooping up the ball. He
was in full stride, his leg pads clicking as he ran and
his sneakers leaving faint damp spots on the floor.

Up over centre floor Nish ran.

Travis was alarmed. Nish had never come out
this far before. If he lost the ball now, they were
sunk.

Sarah and Dmitri were both calling for passes.
One Mini-Rock defender broke off, covering
Sarah, the Owls' most dangerous playmaker.

That left Travis free.

He saw that Nish could see him. He raised his stick, expecting the pass. He barely saw Nish's hand move. The thick goalie glove went up into the pocket and jammed the ball down hard into the crotch of the stick.

Nish faked to Travis, then turned on the only player back. He faked a bounce shot through the player's legs. The defenceman went down to block. Nish threw his goalie stick high in the air, so high it came within a whisker of rattling off the overhead lights that hung from the rafters.

It was as if all time had come to a stop.

Travis could sense the crowd, every eye in the place raised to the heavens as Nish's huge floating, spinning stick went up and over and began to come down.

Nish crashed right through the crouching defender, sending him flying. He reached up with one hand and caught his stick perfectly, placed his other hand up the shaft, and in one motion he shot.

A perfect "Muck Munro"!

The ball bounced once, rattled between the leg pads of the Mini-Rock goaltender, and into the net.

Screech Owls 14, Mini-Rock 13.

Travis's first instinct was to look at the clock. Nothing left, the buzzer already going.

His second instinct was to pile on Nish, who was already down in an accommodating heap.

The Screech Owls had won the championship.

Travis was in the pile. Dmitri was on top of him. Sam, then Fahd, then Sarah.

"*You stink!*" Sarah shouted.

"*Ain't it beautiful?*" shouted Nish.

The floor was filling with players and coaches and managers and officials. Muck was running towards the Mini-Rock net, where the official was just pulling the winning goal out from the netting. Travis saw him speak to the official, who nodded and handed over the ball. Muck took it in both hands, gently kissed it, and then walked over to meet Zeke Fontaine, still heading towards the pile from the bench.

Muck held out the ball for his assistant coach.

The old man looked at it. Travis could see he was weeping.

Muck shook the ball. He, too, was in tears.

The old man took the game ball as if it were the most precious, fragile thing in the world.

In a way, it was. More than thirty years after it should have happened, Muck Munro and Zeke Fontaine had their provincial championship.

24

TWO DAYS LATER, THE SCREECH OWLS ALL WENT
to the cemetery, where little Liam Fontaine
would finally be laid to rest.

The Owls wore their team sweaters and acted
as an honour guard. Muck and Mr. Dillinger
acted as pallbearers.

A priest spoke, but Travis wasn't listening to
what he said. He stood, staring at the freshly dug
grave and the small white coffin, the air heavy
with the scent of flowers, and he wept. He didn't
even bother to wipe away the tears.

He had never known the boy. Liam Fontaine
had been dead for decades before Travis was
even born. And yet Travis couldn't get it out of
his head that they were burying the same boy
he had seen that night as he came home from
the movie.

He knew it wasn't possible. He knew it made
no sense at all. But that was how he felt.

After the priest stopped speaking, they
lowered the coffin, and old Mr. Fontaine leaned
over, placing something down into the grave.

Mrs. Lindsay and Mrs. Nishikawa came along with armfuls of roses, handing one each to the Screech Owls for them to place in the grave.

This was what old Mr. Fontaine had done, thought Travis, maybe leaving an orange lily, and he stood behind Nish and Sarah to take his turn.

Sarah dropped her rose and moved on. She, too, was weeping openly.

Nish dropped his. His face was red, his cheeks burning with tears.

Travis bent to drop his rose on the coffin and realized that it was not a flower at all that Liam Fontaine's father had sent to be buried with the boy.

It was the ball from the championship game.

THE END

THE NEXT BOOK IN THE SCREECH OWLS SERIES

Death Down Under

What is it that a great white shark burps up that attracts the attention of international and Australian police?

The Screech Owls are flying around the world to Sydney, Australia, site of the 2000 Olympics, for an exhibition tournament to promote ice hockey in the sports-mad land down under.

The trip, however, involves much more than hockey. The teams coming to Sydney will take part in the Peewee Olympics – a once-in-a-lifetime opportunity for the youngsters to compete in real Olympic sports facilities.

What will it be for Nish? The pole vault? Synchronized swimming? Beach volleyball?

The Screech Owls are also invited to tour Sydney's magnificent zoo and the world-renowned Sydney Aquarium, where Sarah's interest in bizarre marine biology leads to a field trip in search of an endangered sea horse. A field trip that brings the Screech Owls face to face with Death Down Under.

Death Down Under *will be published by McClelland & Stewart in the spring of 2001.*

THE SCREECH OWLS SERIES